OLD VOLCANO ROAD

Pianta

Cover design and typesetting, Pianta; Cloud photo, David Mark, Pixabay.

Dedicated

to Francis Paul Akamine
and to James "Jimmy" Parker, Jr.

and to all the sisters
who've loved their brothers so much

Acknowledgments

Much gratitude to family and friends, whose strength and beauty always appear in one form or another in my writing. Thank you too to groups like Ukwanshin Kabudan for inspiring people about Okinawa and Uchinanchu culture. Deep appreciation also to Kumu Hula Kapena Malulani Perez and Kumu Hula Ann Lokelani Parker for their continued love and kindness. And a special thank you to Kumu Lokelani for helping me see that a book was possible.

CHAPTER 1

FIRE

Eva glanced in the rearview mirror and accelerated.

No one else was on the road.

She slid the windows down a few inches and took in deep breaths. The white ginger was thick in some spots, but for a long stretch, there was nothing but green alongside the rough expanse of highway. Her hair began to lift in the breeze.

She was far from California, where everything was brittle and now burnt. But here there was also fire, and she could taste it in the vog. Moving up the empty road, she could think of only one thing: how much she wanted her brother to live.

She took a sharp left, nearly missing the turn. Slowing, she pulled into the park, finding a space away from the few cars that were there. It was the afternoon and overcast. To calm herself, she sat for a moment and took in the damp air and the green surrounding her. She opened the windows fully and sat in the quiet. In a few moments the image of her brother Gene's face drifted up in her mind, and her stomach started to roil.

Only a few days ago in California, late in the evening, Eva had slipped into jeans and thrown on a loose cotton shirt. Her hands had small cuts and abrasions everywhere; the heat was taking moisture from everything. Twisting her hair up into a clip, she then checked her wallet for cash. "Prepare for evacuation," the crawler read as it moved across the screen, with rows of shelter and emergency numbers. Eva grabbed the thin sheets of thumbnails for the pizzeria she'd been working on and shoved them in her pack. Friends who were out of town on various holidays and work jaunts were safe; she kept flipping through stacks for what she needed, but she felt calm. *Hope I'm not flammable*, she texted Emi, and Emi replied, *only you can prevent forest fires*, followed by an icon of a bear. A strand of hair slipped beside her face, and she glanced in the hall mirror. Despite her calm, the strain showed.

She kept moving, working her way around the stacks of sketches and canvased frames that lay on her desk and on the floor. She shuffled through a stack of mail and unplugged her laptop, slipping it into its case. Kitty, her calico, kept sleeping on stacks of discarded sketches.

Witch Creek, Harris, Rice, and Poomacha fires
small sticks start to shake from the trees
there's a bruise across the sky
branches crack
and the door keeps blowing open

Her craziness had been coiling up for months. "In your thirties and still chasing jobs," her friends would say over tea, and she would just stare down at the table. She had earmarked tonight to knock out more sketches and post on the neighborhood arts council site. She swung the backpack with the laptop and work papers onto her other shoulder. She gazed around the dimly lit cottage that had been built in the 1940s and sighed. She opened the front door and looked out at the ranch style house that stood in front of hers. No lights on and no dog barking. Her landlord had left hours ago with his pittie in his pickup when the evacuation alert first came out. She closed the door and was glad that she had filled the tank. She was supposed to do drop-offs and pickups all day tomorrow, ferrying between Escondido and La Mesa and then back again.

To her, life appeared on the verge of tipping. Even the palms struggled to hold themselves to the ground, barely making it in the drought with waves of heat rising. She rode the freeways as if everyone were lashed onto the backs of serpents, multi-headed hydras that careened in divergent directions. Commutes felt like wastelands, dotted with sinkholes and carcasses of motor-cides.

Yesterday, she'd driven past a driver who was closing his eyes, his hands gripping the wheel. "Hey," she had yelled. "Hey!" She had to keep surging backwards and forwards to get close to his open window. "Eyes!" Again, she yelled. "Open your eyes!" When he did, he looked terrified, terrified of her and of what he was doing. He sped away, veering to the lane on his right. The adrenaline led her on, and she drove the rest of the way at ninety, her heart beating. She was doing just as he was. Her anger was crossing wires with the anger in the air. She was wired into the circuitry of the freeways and her heart rate wouldn't come down.

The drought was turning them dry, and the fires were on their way.

But tonight, she did as she always did. She focused. *Cat carrier. Water. Good to go.* That would be pretty much it. *And photos.* She let the cat keep sleeping and went to the back bedroom to slide open her closet doors. She rummaged around and pulled out a small photo album next to envelopes of old tax returns. She thought a moment about hauling the returns around with her but thought, *let them burn.*

She glanced at the old radio clock and then shoved the small album in her bag. Two photos slipped out to the floor and she reached for them. One was black and white and yellowing. She stood at age three, in a frilly dress on the lawn outside the small wooden house in Honolulu, and Gene was nine, next to her in cowboy gear. Six years later, they would be without parents and living in their aunt and uncle's house. In the other, Eva was in sixth grade and Gene stood in a baseball uniform with his arm around her. She was squinting, and Gene had a rare shy smile.

a palm leaf
curls in the heat
breaking apart as it falls
the horizon is burning

She slid both photos back into the album and secured it in her pack. The two jugs of water were already in the car, and she slid Kitty into the carrier on the passenger seat. Pulling away, she took a last look at the small cottage and the remaining leaves of the tree scattered in the yard.

Fifteen minutes later she was on the I-15 going eighty until a police car, weaving back and forth across five lanes, herded traffic to the exits. Beyond the next exit, the freeway was closed. She looked ahead and then glanced behind. She couldn't head to the coast either. Del Dios had been shut too. She slowly exited away from the herd, u-turned, and got on the 15 headed south. Again, three exits down, the blue light of a patrol car nudged people off to the nearest off-ramp. It was closed everywhere. Emi was texting her, but Eva kept driving.

In twenty minutes, she was on an exit ramp, but now flames had leapt a small patch of grass on the side of the highway. She and the driver on her right had looked across at each other in slow motion. All he could do was look at her and shrug as he edged his car left, nearly on top of hers because the flames were pushing him across. Everyone just kept moving.

She panicked, hemmed in by the cars jammed full of people. She glanced at the rearview mirror at the lines behind her and moved through two intersections, trying to get away from the pack. The smell of smoke had seeped into the car, and Kitty pressed herself against the carrier door, yowling.

Eva kept turning down darkened side streets; she knew somewhere there was a small hotel hidden on one of them. When she found it, it was lit and packed with cars circling the lot. She murmured to herself and to Kitty and pulled into one of the last spaces. She sat for a moment, hands on the steering wheel, and dropped her head and sighed. She texted Emi, *Won't believe where I am. Fill you in later. Am ok.* She walked into the lobby with a backpack, laptop, with her arms around the carrier, passing families sitting in the lobby with their dogs. Wherever there was an outlet, people were charging their phones.

News streamed by on the lobby TV screen. People were loading and unloading horses at supermarket parking lots. Fire leapt up the hillsides intercut with men standing on their roofs hosing down their houses. Clips of blackened silhouettes that used to be neighborhoods made everyone silent.

everywhere black dust flying

peppering eyes

while searing air compresses itself

under the gray insulation of sky

When she got to her room, it was quiet. Kitty darted from the carrier to beneath the bed. Eva slid into the chilled, taut sheets and slept.

"I'm okay. Don't know if you guys have been watching the news. Fire season over here. Love you." It was almost midnight her time and eight pm in Hilo. She paused, wondering if her brother and sister-in-law would pick up. But no one came on and she slid back down to sleep.

When she got up in the morning, there was no work to go to the next day. She popped open the tin of cat food, dished it out on a paper plate, and slid it under the bed. She pulled a cup of applesauce out of her backpack and kept her eyes on the news. "Stay off the road," a frayed-looking newscaster kept repeating. City and state buildings were closed. The fires were only at 20% containment. Flames in the east were heading west, with burns coming from both north and south directions. She reached for her phone, eyes still on the screen.

"Gene?" Still, no one picked up, and Gene's careful, deliberate voicemail came on.

"Min and I are not able to answer the phone, but please leave your name and number. Thank you very much."

She waited. "Just wanted to be sure you got my message." They were rarely out. "Anyway, don't worry if you see the news. About the fires. I'm okay. Love you."

She checked her texts as clips of the fire moved across the screen. *Back in town. Everybody okay*, Emi had texted.

water lines pulse like dying arteries

buckets of pink retardant

drop from the sky
veins of fire spider inland
as the world watches us burn

Kitty didn't come out from under the bed. A newscaster with dark circles under his eyes reported that half a million had evacuated.

wailing trucks
and charred metal blades
seed themselves
symphonic as an apocalyptic opera

firefighters scorch their lungs
sleepless
as they hold onto the fire lines

Stan, a man she had just stopped seeing, texted the next night to check in on her. Tall, lanky, and monosyllabic, he was sitting in his townhouse in Texas, watching the fires. He'd moved there last year to be closer to his young son. When he left, she hadn't known what to say to him. She thought the move would be good for him and necessary for Chet, his son. The name was vintage, a nod to the guitarist. The breakup with Stan had a graceful, inevitable end. Conversations had started to fade out and attempts to Zoom became awkward. The last one was about his not having much to give; that's what he said anyway. Even in the times he had held her, she felt sorrow, as if a slow-acting anesthesia had filled both their veins. Days drifted between times they saw each other or spoke. Neither had given much, so losing "not much" was okay. He was a reasonable guy, she knew, but it was as if they were both slowly counting backwards from a hundred. She didn't fault him or herself. She texted him an "okay" with a thumbs up, and he replied with a "good."

#

At 60% containment, the hotel started to empty. Traffic was slow, but the groups of cars moved with patience. Faces behind windshields were grateful and somber, eager to get back to homes but humbled by having homes to return to. Everyone drove slowly and even the traffic lights seemed to delay. Her thoughts kept drifting as she drove back, and she barely noticed the lights changing or the flashing reds in sections where the lights were out.

Eva was unloading in the carport when she heard Min's call. The cat was already settled back in the house and looking at her through the window.

"Gene's sick." Min's voicemail was quick and shaky. "Can you come?" There was no preamble or explanation.

Eva's face paled. She set down the water jugs she'd been holding and left the car doors open. She walked into the house and passed the mirror. It was only then that she saw the smudges of ash on her face, arms, and hands. Ash lay over everything in the city—cars, lawns, buildings, whatever had been outside. The smell of smoke penetrated everything. Ash was floating in through the open door and onto the wooden floors. She washed her face and hands, and soot ran down her arms and through her fingers. She was shaking. She patted the white towel against her skin and didn't care about the residue of black that stained it.

Exhausted, she closed the bedroom door and lay upon her bed, watching the ceiling fan whirl above her. Before she left, she had stuck tape all around the gaps between the floor and doors to keep out ash, and now the only moving air came from the slowly rotating fan. Eva lay there and closed her eyes. She started imagining a stream running from the top of her head, through her arms, her legs, her veins. She needed the fatigue to get pulled out of her; otherwise, she'd never leave the bed.

The beep from her phone hit like an egg timer as if she were an egg. She forced herself up, checked her texts, and finished packing what she had just unpacked.

She left Kitty with a friend who had two cats of her own and took the small bag that still held the photos. She put auto reply on all her addresses and got on a plane. A strange mishmash of scenes—the footage of horses boarded in parking lots, plates of room service littering the halls, and Kitty yowling—kept playing in her head. She looked out of the window as she left San Diego below then closed her eyes to sleep.

days pass
as firefighters leave their own homes to glow, darken, collapse

they fight to save the city
returning only to fall
into their narrow cots

having slain
the tetrahedron:
the live body
of fire

CHAPTER 2

THE CUFF

Gene hadn't noticed at first. His body had always ached anyway, even when dulled by coffee and the beer he drank. It was practical but not physical work he did, though some might even say it was soulful. He was a bridge between social workers, their clients, and the county. He was the one they would call if something happened; he was the last person they called, usually to thank. This meant late night hours intermixed with emergencies, court hearings, or preliminary research for custody cases.

"Gene … Gene! That's you. Your line," someone would call across the room.

When he finally got his own office, he would sometimes close the door and wonder why he did what he did. In his 20s, he'd had dreams to be a priest. In his 30s he had given that up and chosen advocacy and community work. He had dark, wide eyes and unruly hair, and his body was lean and muscled from running, working, and coffee. He would let his energy coil up inside him but when that silence was pressed into writing, it produced images, sonnets, and odes to anything—the beach, the stars, the women who were drawn to him. They knew he had kindness. They watched the way he was with his sister. He was patient, kind, and tolerant. They craved that from him even though he couldn't give it to them.

"Another time," he would tell them when Eva was too young or too lonely to be left alone. These girls would cluster around him like thick bamboo groves, wanting to mystify and capture him. They would persist, their hair shifting slightly on their shoulders. They leaned into him when he would speak.

When he transferred from O'ahu to start casework in Hilo, he had a sense of beginning. Honolulu had grown increasingly crammed and chaotic. Hilo was approachable, lush, and quiet but nearly to the point of melancholy. He immersed himself. On his first day, his co-worker Jill smiled as she walked him to his desk, "I'm warning you—it's hard to stay long." Then she turned to him and said, "But we hope you do." Then she handed him a stack of cases.

He researched stacks, argued in hearings, and chased down parents trying to get them to respond to inquiries about their kids. He worked. On a rare night he would remember his love for the world, and he would miss his youth in Honolulu—the nights he would drive full blast in his metallic blue sports car in the company of a beautiful girl, accelerating as he ascended Tantalus. The roof of the convertible would be down, his companion's long hair twisting like a waterspout, and the two felt their souls twisting upward in currents that were both temporary and eternal.

But it was rare now that he would recall these moments; instead, he just sank deeper into work.

"Nothing lasts forever, but Gene has," was what they'd say each year in the Hilo office. Mothers, estranged fathers, juveniles he had advocated for, and family court judges who had seen the hours he put in would pack the offices to celebrate making it through one more year. The protective services office at the top of the stairs filled with people in slippers, shorts, work clothes, and uniforms, and they brought haupia, lau lau, pipikaula, even opihi, which they crowded onto makeshift buffet tables. He'd stand, sipping the beer in his hand, nodding as people came up to him.

"Junior's in college now, Gene," one mother said. Gene would nod. "Thanks so much, yeah?" He always wanted to be somewhere else in moments like that; he would nod with a self-conscious smile. But now in the last few months, there were more difficult days. He'd lay on his bed as if he had been netted and dragged up on shore.

A strange malaise had gradually begun to affect his speech, his thoughts, his walk. He was gray and subdued. His gait sometimes reacted like a reluctant stick shift that might jerk and not shift into place. His spirit and body had somehow been eclipsed. This was not the graceful transit into age, but something dark. No one knew what to call it. His voice, which was so measured and even, sometimes shook. His deliberate, focused gait toward courthouses or up stairs at legislative hearings sometimes swayed or and restarted abruptly. The reliability that he'd always had was now replaced by an unpredictability that detached him from everything he had earned and known. Like volcano land, the green earth of who he was, was mixed with obsidian. Whatever it was, it sealed him tight.

#

As anybody who could see, Eva was very much her brother's sister. It was all still there—despite their being second generation and born and raised in Hawai'i, the Okinawan—Uchinanchu—in them remained: the thick hair, the shape of their eyes, and the yielding to sadness and laughter. They had moods that were dark as much as they were bright. Brothers and sisters in their Ryuukyuu lineage had strong ties. In the archipelago, when a fisherman went out at sea, he took a lock of his sister's hair for a safe return.

That morning she told Gene and Min that she had errands to run and wanted a long drive and that she might just stay up at the Volcano House a couple of days. This gave them space if they needed it.

Eva was close to Min. Her sister-in-law was from Seoul, funny, and thin as paper. She and Gene had been married for over twenty years, and his wife now cared for him full time. Eva had been staying with them for weeks, but as cramped as the three were in the small Hilo house, they still found it easy to be together. Whenever she came back for a visit, the three of them always fell into a rhythm immediately. Her brother was only six years older than she was, but now he was frail, and the couple treated her almost like a daughter rather than a sibling or an in-law.

The day before her drive, Eva took Gene to shop and they steered through the packed aisles, weaving back and forth between rushing people. His gate was unsteady, and he used the cart to anchor him. On the island everyone shopped at the same time and the aisles would be jammed with everyone stocking up with paper goods, rice, packs of meat, rolls, soyu, and Spam. Food and generosity were important, and mealtime was meant for this. Steam lifted up from the rice pots, marinated beef was charred and sliced on the table, and bowls of macaroni salad with smaller dishes of kim chee and pickled ginger weighed down packed lunch tables.

He wavered on his feet, and she feared for him as he tried to navigate the aisles, with families of mothers, kids, fathers, and teens crowding the corridors.

But she couldn't think of this now. In jeans and a light jacket, she got out of her car, and the air was cold. She smelled the vog. As she stepped onto the wooden stairs, she thought of the post-war temporary schools that the islands would build, long shoebox shapes made of rough timber.

When she stepped into the gallery, a woman with long white hair twisted up in a knot, greeted her from behind the counter, where she stood untangling necklaces for the display case. She had a long, delicate face, and she smiled.

"Oh," Eva said, "it's beautiful in here." After twenty years in California, Eva was a tourist in Hawai'i now. It hurt to be nomadic. Rueful, she couldn't ignore that California was now her home, despite drought, concrete, and all. She longed for Hawai'i and its water, but the truth was that she had none of its bloodlines nor its knowledge in her bones. Okinawa was in her blood, but it was like an elusive pool she could never quite reach. No matter how much she read or wanted to go there, she hadn't, and she couldn't lay claim to it. She had no language as a bridge. *Once you lose the language, you are lost.* She took in the fragrance of wood and stalks of ginger someone had clipped and put in jars around the shop, and started looking, for what, she wasn't sure.

Uchinanchu

spread over land masses and oceans:

Perú, Brazil, Bolivia, Argentina, Paraguay, Hawai'i

we are like the languages

we adopted

and our physicality as hybrid

She wanted to go immediately to the gems in the cases, but she staved off her impatience. Instead, she turned to the right to look at the books on Hawaiiana that lined the walls. Small, thin volumes and some rare editions described tattoos, horticulture, cultural practices like lei-making, herbal remedies, and food preparation. She pursed her lips, feeling overwhelmed but then stepped forward toward them. She ran her fingertips lightly over the titles, hoping that if her mind couldn't find a key, her sense of feeling might. She turned to take the room in, but drawn to nothing, she walked through the doorway to see what was next.

She stepped into a large lit space devoted to blown glass sculptures, and they were striking. Some were three to four feet high and volatile in form as if they had shaped themselves in some explosion arising out of the ground. They had streaks of orange, rust, and flecks of red, gold, and bronze, as if fired by Pele herself.

An older couple entered the room. The woman, lean and unpretentious, seemed likely from San Francisco, not LA. Her companion was a few paces ahead of her. He looked rushed and slightly disheveled in a white dress shirt and loosened tie. He held a jacket over his arm. The two entered the room, and they took in their breath at the sight. Eva turned to them as they murmured, "beautiful." The man gave a quick nod to Eva, and he stepped into the next room with its books on native birds and fauna.

The phone in Eva's bag buzzed, but she didn't reach for it. It was probably one of her jobs. "When are you coming back?" She didn't have an answer, and she kept moving, as if the sound were some plane overhead that she had a right to ignore. She knew denial was wrong, but she had no appetite for talk. She had no answers.
Aside from the room for the sculptures, the gallery was modest in size, and there was not much more to see, so Eva moved toward the cases that held the jewelry and precious stones.

There were three narrow cases with contemporary and antique pieces displayed beneath the glass, with wide spaces between them. The first piece that drew her were plumeria earrings that had delicately curved petals, the blossoms the size of dimes. They were antique, a bit battered, with dark spots where they were tarnished, making them more beautiful. She thought of the woman who might have worn them, during the 50s, dancing in the sand or on a lauhala mat in someone's living room. "Waikiki" by Andy Cummings would be rising and falling in the background, with orchids pinned into the French twist of the dancer's hair.

She ran her fingers over the milo bracelets that were in a small basket on one of the cases, ignoring another buzz from her phone. The milo was cream colored with striations of green, and others were coffee colored or a deep chocolate brown.

The woman came by and smiled. "I can show you anything." Eva looked closer as she approached, admiring the sheer silk jacket the woman wore, hand dyed with swathes of teal, tangerine, and a pale, pale pink. When she moved, she looked airy, with soft, wide-legged silk pants that billowed. Eva smiled at her, looked at her silk, and said, "So lovely." Many of those who watched the store looked like beautiful artists.

"Thank you."

Eva looked down at her own worn-out running shoes and jeans. She then looked over the glass, motioning. "Could I see this?"

"Sure." The woman unlocked the case and slid the tray out and laid it in on the glass. "This?" she pointed.

"Yes." Eva looked closer. The cuff was antique silver with raised silver lotuses. The lotuses were fully opened, and their stems, as if residing below water, curved back and forth like the infinity sign and the tail of a coiling snake. Its strength struck her, and after she bought it, she slipped it on her wrist immediately, before she even left the store. The woman working in the shop looked at her as she left, and Eva noticed that her eyes were extremely bright and shiny. It made Eva think of an intensely sea with small, peaking waves tipped with silver.

When she walked out of the gallery, she wasn't sure what to do. The day was typical Hilo gray, contrasting with shocks of chartreuse from the hapuʻu growing beside the gallery. She hadn't found anything that she had really come for, even though she had driven with such purpose. She got back into the car and looked outward. She saw a few tourists drift in and out of the lot. It was excruciating to feel time tick by while her brother lay in the dark pool of what was draining life from him. She sat as if waiting for someone.

A half hour drifted by, and a family of five emerged from a large van, and the parents were sunburned pale pink. Their children looked about primary school age and one was in his teens. The kids were laughing and boisterous but became hushed as they passed her car. There was something in her they could sense, something about her that had the sense of mission or grief.

In that moment, she knew she had to drive to the summit. There was no one that she could wait for. If she had been near water, she would have gone to the gods who dwelled there. But she was here now, and she had to go where she could.

She had to go as a foreigner, a fake, a displaced soul. She hadn't given time to be like those who had always been here. With no blood quantum, language, or traditional ties, she was a stranger. Fear ran through her, for herself and Gene. That fear made her angry, and that anger made her reckless. She turned the key and headed up the road, but this time toward the vents where the sulfur was rising. She would head to the top.

CHAPTER 3

COMING TO

When Eva came to, she shifted slowly. Her arm hurt and was twisted. She adjusted her eyes to the light. The last thing she remembered was the art gallery in the rearview mirror and her accelerating up through the o'hia and fern. Then nothing.

She lifted herself up slightly, but then breathed in sharply. Her shoulder ached and she could only sit. She couldn't stand. What she could see was that she was in a long black tube, and it was damp. She breathed in air that felt stagnant and cold.

Eva was dizzy but didn't feel afraid. She sat up, then shifted over a couple of feet to find something to lean against. The old reflex to what she was taught, even at this moment, made her want to leave any growth, however small, undisturbed. She took the least amount of surface she could to avoid contact with whatever grew on the curving walls. Wherever she was, it felt like a sacred space.

At this moment, she thought about what she often felt—caught between worlds. Her internal life filled her, buoyed her, insulated her, refined her, but she was often still so precarious in the outside world. She felt like a small scrap of fabric pinned to a line that that held her to earth, but at any moment that line could break.

There didn't seem to be a singular logic to these wild, varying moments. For all the scary moments, there was also the beautiful. One night, when she was twenty, she sat as her mother swept up her hair and in it, pinned a dozen small gardenias that she had picked from the yard. That night, she and her boyfriend stood above on a circular arena balcony watching a weary Eric Clapton play "Layla" live. She remembered looking around the haze of smoke and lights, taking in the heavy scent of gardenia as the guitar solo vibrated in her chest. *How does this all fit into a life?*

Now through habit, she leaned against the wall and closed her eyes. *Sometimes nothing fits.* She didn't know for how long or how deeply she might be in this moment, so she just closed her eyes and let go.

#

Some days Gene moved through the days as if he were pulled so deep below the water, too far below to come up again, but somehow, he could still breathe.

"Calls for you." A staffer would waive a stack of pink message slips, after he'd return from long drives to Kona to help that office when they were shorthanded. He'd grab them and go through them, his voice deliberate and patient while his plate lunch would sit, uneaten.

At the end of the day, he and others used to peel off toward home or have a beer in the little bar around the corner. Jill would make them laugh with reenactments of the day's snafus, and Gene would sit in the corner, sipping his beer, occasionally chuckling but with his eye on the clock to head home.

Now he would only stay till lunch, and when home, he slept for long periods of time. It was as if that were his one true relief. Sleeping did not require going anywhere or explaining to crying clients why regaining custody of their kids wouldn't be possible just yet. The stack of messages grew until they were eventually being diverted off to others in the office.

But now there were new things on the list, like finding ways to walk in a steady gait or keeping his stamina for a day. He had stopped driving three months ago when his reaction time had slowed. On the days he would come to work, Jill and another staffer would stop by the house. Animated and full of chatter, they would offer him an arm to lean on if he needed it to get to the car.

It was as if creatures had risen up from several layers above hell to put their talons into him, growing closer to the surface of the living. He focused on work in the day, but at night he would sleep uneasily, his body more keenly aware of them. Immersed in dark water, these long bodies swam with their wings folded against them like swans They moved in pods of three or more, and the water itself was a thin black, but the red of the creatures' skin glittered beneath. They moved as if they could easily fly up and out of the water, their tails rippling behind them. There was a rasping sound that surrounded their wings and the hiss of steam as their heated bodies made contact with the water.

A gap had formed between his life and his body, and he didn't know how to bridge it.

He had been lonely this morning when Eva had left the house. She had rested her hands on his shoulders and said, "Love you," as she left the table. Min was washing the dishes in the kitchen, and she waved as Eva pulled out from the driveway.

He sat with the local paper, and the paperwork he had to do. He no longer had cases of his own now, but he helped his office with piecemeal paperwork. He didn't miss the tragedy of the cases, but he missed the activity of the office, the sense of helping people with what they needed and the pace of change, the rush of people coming in and out.

I had to loosen the cord
from my father and mother

a knot that gets untied
like the anchor rope
that disintegrates
into filmy seaweed from years
of lying at the bottom of the sea

Even though his sister was a few years younger, Gene had always seemed much older. They had lost their parents when he was fifteen and she was nine, and they had been raised by their father's aunt and uncle, who cared for them but who had always been very reserved.

It had fallen to him to tell Eva when their parents didn't return one night.

After a long silence, his father's uncle told him on the phone. "Heart attack. Your mom went into the water too."

Eva didn't look at Gene's face when he told her. He stood in the doorway, and she remained seated on the floor, leaning against her bed. His eyes became full and still, and they didn't change after that. The weight of their grief became part of him, and the silence that he had always had deepened. Years later in the courthouse, when he would speak for warring families and their children, his compassion made people pause. His demeanor was even but, as one judge remarked, his preparation unyielding.

The aunt and uncle had no children of their own, but they weren't worried about caring for the two. Gene had always been quiet and responsible, and more so after the parents' death. Eva drew inward and fell into the silence of their home. Their uncle died early at fifty-two, and the aunt lived not much longer. Eva and Gene were always on their own. They sat in the quiet of the spare and simple house in Mo'ili'ili, shaded by the mango tree thick with pollen and fruit. They worked without speaking, preparing themselves for life on their own outside the screen doors.

Eventually, Gene thought less and less about beautiful things, and then only about social work cases. His time was spent sorting out custody hearings, verifying or disputing charges, or testifying for wards of the state. In his emails with Eva—he didn't like texting or calling—they didn't communicate about work. They never spoke about their loss, but the heaviness clung to Eva, and she would try to counter it. "You're so responsible," she would laugh, "compared to me!" Whenever she came to visit, she hugged him, joked, and told him she loved him. Now she drove him to appointments to see doctors and specialists, sitting with him as he waited.

That morning after breakfast and after Eva drove off, he said, "I'm tired," and returned to the bedroom; he told Min, it was to read, but it was really to sleep. He knew it was odd to sleep against the sun; the nights should have been for sleeping, and as he dreamt in daylight, his hands kept grasping at his throat as if to pull something away that prevented him from breathing. He slept but uneasily, teetering on the edge of something he was on the way to reach.

"It's loss of control, Gene," the therapist had once told him, "We can't always control what happens to us."

Gene looked at her. *I never thought control was ever possible,* he thought.

#

Eva didn't know how long she'd been sitting with her eyes closed, but her body was stiff, and her eyes had difficulty opening and adjusting to the light. She then heard her name spoken very, very softly.

"Eva."

It was as if she'd never heard her name before. The sound was as soft as touch. The space warmed itself and hummed. Her name became softer and softer until it was so silent that it became a light, and that light permeated her. It soaked into her and she felt herself move, rocked, like one would soothe a baby or like the gentlest lapping of water around the shell of a boat. The rocking continued and expanded, and she was drifting and immersed. It was as if she could be there for hours, days, weeks.

Slowly, the motion started to subside, and gradually, everything was still again. Slowly she opened her eyes. As she did, everything glowed, golden and warm. She had to blink for her eyes to adjust to the intensity of the light. She sat, still seated, and quiet. The light had soaked into her bones and the marrow in them was now like a green liquid that ran through her and the earth: alive, urgent, and fluid, with the ability to nurture everything that was parched and weak, not just in her but in everything around her.

She sat. She took it all in, a little shaky. Then her breath started to tremble and vibrate, and she started to pant, and a force of siphoning air moved through her head and then her nostrils. Her body shook with intense breathing. Her body had the fire of light and air in a single current. She stayed seated, lightheaded, and when she looked up despite the darkness, she could see herself at the center, like the hub of a wheel with spoke-like rays spreading outward in a great circumference. Wobbly, she could barely take it all in.

There was no sense of time. She didn't know how long it continued, whether it was a day, a night or a moment. She couldn't tell. Her breathing had gradually slowed like music that was ending then fading off. As a teen, she'd learned the practice of meditation and had different perceptions and experiences, but this felt new.

"You can't stay here. You need to come this way."

Eva had closed her eyes and was still resting against the cave wall. She tried to open her eyes but against a light so bright that she closed them again. Unsteady, she tried to get up but couldn't.

"Take your time."

She kept trying to open her eyes. She was suddenly so tired, as if she could sleep for days or weeks. *Can't rush,* she told herself. She wanted to cry. Then anger started rising up in her. It was the same anger that rose when she had to force herself to get up and work fifteen-hour days, driving to the 13,000 part-time jobs she had. She sat still. *I'm not getting up.*

After a while, she shifted. The dizziness increased then subsided. Then she realized that this intense bright light made her body warm and fluid again, rather than bruised and cramped. Still, she sat, resolute. *I'll sit until I'm ready.*

Her body became quiet again.

She opened her eyes slowly, sometimes blinking to adjust. In front of her she saw a diffusion of light with no defined lines but roughly in the shape of a robed figure. The light said, "Come now. You can't stay here." The light then turned and moved forward, glancing backward occasionally as if to reassure her, and Eva followed.

She and the cloak of light moved down the passageway, but Eva couldn't see clearly.

She didn't know it then, but as the two waited by the stone doors of the great hall, her hosts were gathering. They began to sit in two rows of a half circle, about forty feet across. Each row had its own tier. The tiers had tall chairs, some of which looked wooden, others alabaster, and other unknown, but they were all a creamy white. Those sitting in the chairs were light beings, but their forms weren't clearly defined. She didn't know if they were male or female; all seemed to have forms like cloaks, and these were not clearly discernible shapes. Instead, they and the objects in the room were very soft, diffused, without sharp edges.

The doors opened and Eva heard a rustle as she and her guide stood in the entryway facing the two tiers of her hosts. Still lightheaded, Eva kept following closely behind her guide.

She felt nervous but also had the same feeling when she was first in the cave. She heard a murmur that wasn't her name but that felt like it was. It was so comforting and quiet that when that sound became silent, it became light. She turned to look at her guide, who gestured that she continue alone, and she did, walking down the long middle aisle toward the tiers. As she walked to meet her hosts, she thought she was doing fairly well, without shaking.

Time shifted in ways she couldn't measure. How long it might take to cover a distance couldn't be gauged. Her heart felt full, and her attention spread everywhere. Grateful, she enjoyed everything even though there was really nothing to see. She moved through hazy air as if she were seated in a plane passing through clouds, but it was also soundless, pure, gentle.

When she made it all the way down the aisle, she approached a curve of seven seats that faced the tiers, but they were empty. She chose a chair directly in the middle, with three empty on each side. She was suddenly grateful to sit. When she sat, she realized that the light rustling sound had stopped, and the entire room quieted even further, and she sat and closed her eyes. It calmed her. The room then became even more still, and she released a long breath. Her body relaxed and her breathing became lighter. Then as she often did, she lost track of time. She slipped deeper and deeper past everything. Past the room, past the beings, past her chair and the tiers, she slid, feeling so humbled that tears began to fall from her eyes.

#

At the house, Gene wasn't doing well. He began to twist and turn, and he continued grasping at his neck. The two Shih Tzu-poodle mix pups kept raising their heads, whimpering sometimes, licking his arm to reassure him and themselves that it would be okay. His body was hot and his mouth dry. His eyelids fluttered as he lay in the bed.

After glancing through the jalousies in the kitchen, Min ran outside to bring in the clothes on the line. The sky was darkening. She wanted to weed the small patch of green onions, cilantro, cabbage and chili peppers at the side of the house. She knew he was sleeping, so she

39

hurried to finish the things she needed to do. She looked up at the heavy gray clouds and rushed even more; when it rained like this, the drops were heavy, as big as Job's tears, and everything would stay damp for days. She dropped the laundry into the basket and decided to forgo the weeding. It was starting to rain.

CHAPTER 4

THE PURGE

Just days before the fire, Eva had been in California in the middle of a crusade to clear out her cottage. She had hauled out boxes from her closet and cleared out boxes of old work—drafts of stories, poems, old paintings and sketches she had kept for years.

The rain hits the street

like a million spiders scrambling for holes.

"Looking at this stuff hurts," she told a friend over tea, "or maybe I should laugh. Maybe they're just thoughts of a stranger who's lost in whatever moment there is. What do you do with all this?"

Last night I dreamt of Phillip Seymour Hoffman. He was with me in Hilo. He had just passed away from a drug overdose, and we walked arm in arm. You could see the thin wisps of his hair and his pale skin; there was so much light, as if he were nearly transparent. Only his wool coat was dark. Each task seemed to test and hurt him.

After hours of sifting through boxes of notes and stacks of sketches and thumbnails, she realized her life could be divided into the categories she had made: "keep," "toss" or "shred."

I can write this poem

but I can't find a better place to live

I hear Sanskrit on the subtle

but my yard is full of weeds

I'm in sweatpants 24/7

I look a mess

worn out from surly people

even "hello" can set someone off!

Going through this was like seeing a parade of her life—where it was going and where it wasn't. By now she had submitted sketches and portfolios to most places in town, and the places she could for writing. She freelanced at four to five places, all part-time. Months ago, a friend sat with her over tea, staring downward as she listened to Eva. "You're burning out," she said.

"I only know about working hard, not working smart. I've never been clever," Eva said, glancing down at her cup.

"I'm worried about you," her friend replied. "Change or be changed, Eva."

#

It was time. Eva drew her attention back in. She was in the hall with the hosts now, and she was ready.

She tilted her head to the right slightly, and the light in the hall began to intensify. This is how perception starts. If quiet enough on the inside, she might be able to see and hear.

CHAPTER 5

THE QUESTION

No one spoke, and she couldn't hear audibly, but she could feel the question from her hosts.

"Do you know why you're here?"

She didn't know what to say. Instead, she wanted to run all the pictures in her head past her hosts. She had pictures and film and emotions in her head but no words.

"Can you look without me saying?" she asked.

She closed her eyes to keep a deeper focus. She focused on her brother. She had images in her head of him walking her to school when her parents first died, his talking with her when she was a teenager, and the deaths of their guardian aunt and uncle. She thought about the years she and Gene had argued. This life unreeled in front of her, the fighting about the work he did, the relationships she had, the money neither of them had. She thought too of the quiet scenes of them reconciling, the long letters they wrote to each other, the emails between Hawai'i and California, and the illness that now held Gene. These images shifted in color from sepia, sometimes black and white, and sometimes vivid color. They flew through her head rapidly, like spools of film escaping from a reel, with bright flashes of projector light interspersed.

When she was finished, she opened her eyes, relieved. Whatever happened, she had conveyed to them who he was and what he meant to her. Whatever happened, someone else knew about the love they had and what strength he had given her.

That meant something.

Then other moments began to flood into her. Once he parked the roadster sideways into the garage just to see if he could make it fit. On another day he chased her around the house after she had taped over the bathroom door with newspaper to seal him in. She thought of the weekend of shaving cream fights when their aunt and uncle were off island. This was the Gene that so few saw. Someone playful, impulsive, and funny, untethered to the weight of duty. Her last image of him was of that perfect summer—the clear bay that he took her to with their friends early in the morning. They would float on rafts or lie on the empty beach, leaving only when crowds started arriving.

She found herself bowing her head in gratitude. She found the words. "This is why I'm here."

The hosts began to rustle, and she realized that it was more like air moving or the faintest feeling of wind but much, much softer. She waited.

"We know why. We're helping you."

"It's that fast?" she asked. "Then I didn't have to come?" she asked.

"No, no," they laughed. "Don't get mad," one said, and they laughed more.

I don't know how it works, she thought. "No, but it works anyway," they said. "Here, take this." They tossed her the image of thin mesh links that could be worn as armor. She slipped it over herself, and she saw it covered her body.

"This will help him," they said, and they tossed a deep blue robe to her. "It'll soothe him." In her mind, she gathered the cloak to carry with her.

Then with the last gift, she was startled but curious.

They handed her a broom.

"Sweep out those thoughts," they said and laughed. Then, "Okay, forget the broom," and they laughed again.

With each object, she thanked them, and they told her to thank the highest beings, and filled with gratitude, she did.

She wondered why their response to her requests for help was so different. In her mind she began to see all the times she'd been so mad and disappointed. So many times, she had seen suffering, and she hadn't been able to do anything about it. She had asked for help so many times, when she was a kid and when her parents were both gone, and now with Gene; she had begged for help, but who had come?

Her anger at those times wasn't just about loss. It was about the way of suffering.

"I've seen good things happen to bad people, and bad things happen to good people," she'd written one night. "Life can ripple out like strings of math equations, triggering events that no one mind can know."

She thought of those she'd loved, lost, missed—even of the animals she had nursed through healing. Some had made it, others had not. People were supposed to think, when it's time, it's time. All living things, at some point, suffered. But she would still get angry. Once a stray lay in her arms, panting, and she ran from the house down the street to her car, but the scrawny cat died in her arms before she could get help. She was furious.

Her faith could fly off like an errant kite that gets tangled in electric lines or lost in a crash somewhere in a stranger's lawn. Those times, she wanted to scream and grab help, as if she could, from the air. Her steadiness could be taken away by these gusts, unexpected, always in a storm.

In these times, a kind of darkness would come around. This was the gap she would fall into and struggle to climb out of. It was the same darkness that made her want to give up, that made her feel that Gene wouldn't get better. This was not prudent due diligence or an inevitable uncertainty that was always there in life. This was something else entirely. If this came upon her, she would have no energy to press against grief, fear, or doubt, or even the judgments she made against herself. *What if this doesn't work?*

She pulled herself together and focused on where she was and what surrounded her. She focused on the images that had just flashed through her head. She focused on Gene, and her saying "Love you" as she left the house this morning. She breathed deeply. It was if she simply stepped back, away from a sliding cliff.

If we can choose what is real, she thought as she faced her hosts sitting in tiers, *I choose this.*

She felt assent rising in her chest. With that, two robed beings on either side of her accompanied her out of the hall, and she knew that it was time to begin. More lay ahead of her, the hosts knew, but letting her know too much might not work to her advantage, but she knew enough to keep going.

#

Before all of this, on many days, no one needed to tell her about her life in the city, where she really was or what she was surrounded by. She knew enough; it was a level of hell, even if she was on earth. If she could not smell the dark, she could see it and feel it. It was strange. It was despair, violence, fear, or apathy. It had a ferociousness or a paucity of emotion. It strangled or starved one. It could drip, drip, drip the life out of one's hope. It took time and wasted it. It ran parallel to life and then diverted it like sludge being poured down a sink.

Those times she felt fear. She believed in the prevalence of light, but she also knew that the more the light rose, the more battles between light and dark might appear. The dark was challenged by light.

But she focused despite all. She did her due diligence. She cultivated a sense that all things—no matter how extraordinary—were ordinary. She paid her bills and followed rules, like turning on her signal even if no one else was on the road. She kept her life modest, avoided making big claims, and paid off debts when she fell into them. From the outside, all such lives look ordinary, but on the inside, *What exists in all of us*, she would think. *What sorrows get built into all those hollows*, she thought, *as we try so hard to retain our space in the world*.

But on the very good days, on the days she was clear, and on the days that good things ruled, she felt light. And beyond everything that was external, she had the internal world. Life was agile and frictionless within: electrifying, silent, and quick. Problems could be identified and fixed with a thought or intention. There were things to combat, but there could be certainty and recovery. The hosts saw this in her. Anything good could happen in this world.

But the physical world had its grim practicalities: freeways, contentious people, time-consuming minutiae of the mundane, and as in both worlds, beasts.

The real test would be to bridge this all. She would have to hold onto both worlds to make it. Some days she didn't know if she could. It was like a globe that was split in half and rotating on two different axes at once, with someone asking, "Can you explain?"

I have no answers for how this will work, she told herself, *especially when I am who I am. I'm not strong enough, and I am so tired*.

She'd text between stops. *Just driving endlessly. Laundry, bookshelves, cleaning the fridge. Tick tock. No time*.

The physical world had clocks, and clocks in this world mattered. But the events of the day would become indistinguishable—just a long string of events, like time lapse photography of seeds growing, blooming, then expiring.

"Who has time to sort this out?" she'd written once in a post. "There is no time to think anymore. No time to drift like a fatalist or recede like a nihilist. All we can do is act and hold onto whatever threads there might be to hold onto. And be grateful for that."

"I'm not a healer," she remembered telling the hosts before she left the hall. "I don't know how to heal, but I can look for those who do."

#

Grateful for the light again, she thought of what the hosts had given her. She shook her head when she thought of the broom. She smiled.

"It's funny to be known so well," she told them.

It was a big step for her to let others so completely in her head. It felt scary; it felt like a relief. But that's what it's like in desperate times. She wanted to laugh thinking of the things she used to worry about, like finding parking, the mess of a house she lived in, or what she could live on if she lived to be ninety. Or of what people thought about her work, her choices, or what went on inside her. All that seemed unimportant. Her mind had grown so quiet when she had been in the great hall. She wanted to keep that with her. She carried all that they had given within her. She started to feel alive. She knew now she had a way to help Gene.

CHAPTER 6

THE CORRIDOR

The great hall was behind her, and she was alone now, making her way down the corridor. The guides had given her a torch when she had left the gathering of the hosts. To get to what she needed, she'd have to go through the way she had come. Love had rushed through her heart when the guides had looked at her to say goodbye. When they looked at her that way, she didn't feel afraid. In that last moment before setting out alone, she let them see everything in her mind. What they saw were clips of movie film that flew in the air. Who she was was still being assembled as if in a giant editing room. She was afraid of what they might see, but she also wanted them to see. She was afraid of exposure, but she couldn't afford to have anything hidden. If they missed something, this could bring failure. Losses like these are irreparable. *You have nothing to lose when you're about to lose what matters.* But she curbed those thoughts. This was no time to be reckless.

Problem one, she thought as she stepped further down the corridor. She noticed that there was now a downward slant on the earth beneath her. She was now descending, no longer walking on level ground. She also started to smell an acrid odor, and the air was much more moist and damp. She looked down, glad she had her old walking shoes; she had been sheepish about them when she had seen the beautiful woman in the gallery because she had looked so scruffy when the woman had been so elegant. But now she was grateful for being dressed as she was. Still, she didn't feel prepared as the ground grew softer, grittier, then muddier.

The torch felt heavy, and the radius of light it gave was wide. She had been walking at a good clip, but she started to slow. The ceiling began to lower, and it was getting harder to hold up the torch. She started to hear water moving and the hiss of steam. The ground grew wetter, and her stomach was uneasy.

She paused and closed her eyes for a moment. She wanted the torch to create a ball of light around her. Opening her eyes, she glanced down at the lotus cuff that circled her wrist. Then stepping forward, she began picking up her pace, asking that light expand in all directions. She took a deep breath and released it, thinking of Gene and of light everywhere. Covering ground quickly, she stepped forward and saw the narrow corridor had abruptly opened up to a large pool and a high ceiling. Suddenly, she heard a great whoosh and boom, the way a fireball ignites because of a sudden accelerant.

A giant cluster of red, liquid-dripping creatures began to fly up out of the pool in front of her. Triggered and terrified, she yelled, charging toward them as if she could scare them off like pigeons. Squawking, they swooped up in clusters of three or fours, and she realized there were hordes of them. The cave had a ceiling, scores of feet high, and the creatures were now spreading everywhere. Some were still leaving the water, but many were now midair above the pool, crashing into each other as they were all trying to take flight, rising up to get away from what they couldn't see. She could see now they were eyeless; she whooped as she ran and her torch flamed up. She kept backing up then charging toward them, with so much force that she nearly ran into the pool herself.

All the while the creatures were crashing into each other in their attempts to fly up at once, their tails whacking and bruising each other, and their long necks ungainly in the cramped space of the cave. They couldn't gain enough air space to open their wings, and they began to fall. Just as they did, embers from Eva's torch fell into the water, and the booming sound began again. Then as if the pool were gasoline, the embers bloomed and ignited, flaming up at the bodies in the sky. Their skins had been drenched in the pool, and like fireworks, their bodies began to combust, their flesh charring and turning to ash.

She could hear the boom of the flames, the attempts of their flapping wings, the smell of steam and flesh mixing, hissing, and the air moving at great speeds with falling cinders. Eva immediately backed up, away from the water and returned to the narrow passageway. She curved her back against the cave wall as the ash rained.

In his sleep, Gene shook and his muscles burned. Whatever had seeped into him was being cooked out of him. He broke into a heavy sweat and then fell into a deeper, more settled sleep.

Eva couldn't stay where she was, afraid to be trapped in the narrow passage. She had to edge around the perimeter of the pool to get to the much larger passageway on the other side. She sidled along the pool, avoiding the falling debris until she could start running, covering her mouth to keep from breathing in the air. The pool was becoming dark sludge, with ash and remains having fallen into the water. After she had made her way completely around the pool, she shook like a dog after a bath. She wanted to fling anything off that may have touched her. She thanked the light and asked that the water be made clear and bright again. She then turned away from the pool, continuing on the cave corridor. Behind her there were sweeping sounds and sizzling as if rain were hitting hot asphalt, and while the steam cleaned the air, the sludge became more viscous, spreading as it went.

CHAPTER 7

TO THE WATER

Slightly dizzy, Eva struggled with her balance but kept moving. The torch seemed to buoy her. Holding it seemed to lift her up, rather than weigh her down. She started running. The cave corridor seemed to curve, sometimes sharply, and she just kept following along the walls. She saw the ground was increasingly solidified with pahoe'hoe. Despite the unevenness, she tried to keep her speed. It reminded her of the sprints she would sometimes do along the coast in California when the air was very clean, and when there were no mothers with baby carriages or bicyclists, but just the occasional walker that she could easily run around. The water would be to her right, and she would run, smelling the eucalyptus, the brush, and the sea water. Although the oncoming coast road traffic was to her left, the cars driving past her seemed to fuel her. She thought of that coast as she ran, and she lost track of time as she kept ascending at a gradual incline until coming to a fork, where, without stopping, she decided in a moment to take to the right.

She kept up her pace, and as she did, she let herself just listen to the sound of her running, and the sound of the torch as it moved in the air. The flame fluttered softly, as gently as her breath, and that kept her steady until she noticed another sound growing beneath it. Then she realized the air was opening up, feeling cleaner, fresher and familiar. It was the sound and smell of the ocean that was she was running to. She had chosen the correct path. Now there was a steep decline. Her pace started to slow. It grew steeper until she had to stop. The path had ended, facing a sharp turn downwards. She winced. She would have to partially slide the next twenty feet or so, which meant not only scrapes, but also disturbing whatever micro-growth there was on the walls. At the very bottom, it opened, and she could see sunlight coming through. She had nearly made it to the outside. She hesitated, then stopped. She lowered the torch, snuffing out the flame on the cave floor. Not waiting for it to cool, she slipped it through a loop on her pack. There was enough light to see, and the wall was steep. She slipped the lotus cuff off her arm and into her back pocket to protect it from being battered or scraped. Then she started, half sliding her way down.

She struggled to find edges to grip, and the rock was damp, slippery and sharp. She took her time. But as she slid and inched downward, the light increased, and there were more crevices that she could use for traction. She thought she could hear the ocean.

Eva finally made her way to the bottom. She didn't want to look to see what she had just left. Thrilled with the increased light and the smell of the air, she thought she heard waves. She let go of the last grip and foothold and slid the rest of the way. She hit the ground and her legs gave out for a moment, spent. She could breathe the ocean and smell the air. After a moment, she stood up, brushed herself off and checked her scrapes. Then feeling around in her back pocket, she slipped the cuff back on. She ran her fingers over the lotuses and thought of Gene.

Once her eyes adjusted to the light, she saw that she had made it to water. About thirty feet ahead, the cave opened. Eva could see the shore, and she took a quick intake of breath. Her eyes struggled to adjust but she saw, with relief, it was low tide. The water had pulled back from the glittering black sand, leaving the green strands of limu exposed, and the tide pools bare.

As Eva adjusted to the light and began to make her way out, she noticed to the far right, the back of a woman standing out in the low tide, looking out to the ocean. Her waist long hair, full and wiry, lifted in the wind. She stood, wearing a loose white t-shirt with a faded red pareo wrapped around her waist and hips. She turned, looking at the ground, then headed toward the cave.

Without thinking, Eva stepped back out of the woman's line of sight, against the wall of the cave as if she had been intruding. Then she recovered herself, and as the woman stood at the front of the cave, Eva stepped forward.

The woman walked in, unsure, adjusting to the light. She held back, but then stepped toward Eva. "You don't recognize me?"

Eva hesitated. The woman had big, dark eyes and long lashes. She had high cheekbones and light skin with freckles, and her lips were full and smiling. Although she had stood looking out at the shore in what seemed a poignant stance, she smiled sweetly now, and her arms reached out to embrace Eva.

"You don't recognize me, huh? I'm not that old!" She walked closer to Eva. "I am so glad to see you."

Eva stepped toward her, saying, "Lia?" "Oh, man. It's you!" Eva reached for her and the two embraced. "It's been a million years."

Eva had tears on her face, and Lia did too.

Eva moved to go out toward the sun, but Lia held her arm. "No, Eva, we need to stay in here for a while. Let's talk."

Lia slipped her arm through Eva's, and said, "So good to see you. So good to see you." She moved Eva closer to the opening of the cave, and they sat on two flat rocks. "Let me see you first."

She laughed. "Wow, Eva, man, we're old! How long has it been?"

Eva looked at her and laughed. Lia had always been beautiful, kind and funny. They had been part of a group of friends, kindergarten through high school. After high school, the group dissolved, and they went in different directions. A year or two later, Eva left for California for school and then work, and she hadn't been able to come back to live. Lia had stayed in Hawai'i and helped her family. Her mother, father, and sister had gone through illnesses. In the beginning they had tried to write, but Eva had kept moving and changing addresses. It was such a different life that she couldn't explain. Throughout, Lia had taken care of her family; this was how it could be with island life. They hadn't seen each other for years.

They hugged each other again, and Eva's arm slipped through Lia's, as they sat on the stones. They became quiet, and Lia looked up again out toward the waves.

"Listen," Lia said. "I need your help," and she looked again at the sea. "I love someone."

"I'm so happy for you! You deserve it," and Eva hugged her again.

Lia was quiet. "I'm waiting for him here."

Eva was silent. She didn't know what that meant.

"I'm already here," Lia repeated. "I'm just waiting for him now."

Eva began to understand, and she began to cry.

"It's okay, sister," and she put her around Eva, with Eva's head bowed. "I'm good, I'm so good. It's so much better for me. You'll see someday. It's good. You'll see. Hey, I'm always going to look this way. I'm never getting old," and she laughed.

Eva half laughed and half cried.

"Good," Lia laughed, "Don't waste time, right?"

"Okay," Eva said, nodding, wiping the tears off her face. "Don't waste time."

"That's right," Lia said, and a sweet sadness passed over her face for a moment. "And it's no big thing," she said. "Just need to wait for him here, okay," and she paused, "you need to go out there. You've got to help Gene, right?" and she smiled.

"Right," Eva said, nodding.

"So I'm good, you're good, and it's all going to be good," and Lia wrapped her arm around Eva again and squeezed her tight.

"That's right," Eva said, smiling and tearing, "it's all good."

"I just wanted to see you and tell you that," Lia said. "We never forget, and we always have the same good feeling. That's why I'm waiting here for the one I love, and that's why you're going out there. That's all I wanted to tell you."

"I know," Eva said, nodding.

"So I'll be here, and if you come back before he comes here, I'll be waiting," and she looked Eva in the eyes. "But if I'm not, you're going to be okay anyway, right? Gene's going to be all right too. I know now. I know how it works. It all works out."

Eva smiled at Lia. Her face was beautiful and her eyes were so deep and bright. "Good times ahead, man!"

"That's right," Eva said, nodding.

"Just do me this one thing," Lia said. "You take care. That's what you can do for me. Take care. What we feel lasts forever. Know that, okay?" She looked at Eva.

"I got it," Eva said, and hugged Lia.

"So you go now, okay? I'm going to wait here," Lia walked Eva out. "The tide's coming in, so you have to go."

The two women stood and hugged, and the tide started to wash in. Eva started to walk away but then turned back. "Take this," and she started to undo the torch on its loop. "Easier for him to find you. Just in case." Lia smiled at her, hugged her, and said, "I won't need it. He'll find me. You take it. You'll be out in the world."

They hugged each other again, and Eva walked away, looking back and waving, and then she headed over the sand, along the shore, feeling grief and gratitude at the same time.

CHAPTER 8

FULL MOON

Min wasn't sure what to do; Gene was sleeping, but he had broken out into a heavy fever and deep sweats. She had tried to waken him and ask him if he needed the doctor, but he hadn't answered. She knew anyway that he wouldn't want to go. He had started to feel depressed about the visits to the doctors and hospital. They were kind, and they had helped in other ways, but in this case, they didn't know what to say. He started to feel the need to just rest, to be away from everyone. He was comforted by home and the pups, and by Min herself, who would let him sleep or wake up at odd hours to give him soup or sit by him if he couldn't sleep.

It had also started to rain, big heavy sheets of rain and wind, and she did not want to make it down the winding road to town and the clinic. It wasn't that she didn't want to make the effort; it was that she felt so much safer here, and he did too. Their lives had started to change because of the darkness, but the house still radiated something good and strong.

She looked out the glass doors, and the baskets of laundry she had pulled in before the rain started and she decided to wait. She would see how he was. She would give him time before she would try to take him to town. In the meantime, the dogs had woken, and they ran to her, whimpering to be fed, and that comforted her. She talked to them, admonishing them to slow down as they ate while Gene kept sleeping as it rained.

When Gene finally did wake, he had difficulty opening his eyes. Drenched in sweat, his eyes were heavy. He moved his limbs slowly in case the dogs were sleeping next to him, but they weren't. He didn't hear the sound of rain, which surprised him, and the room was very cold. Like Eva had done, he sat up very slowly and gradually opened his eyes.

He wasn't sure at first where he was. He called out for Min and for the dogs, but no one came. It was dark, and he reached for the table light, but the lights didn't go on. A bit of panic rose up in him and he swore, but then he stopped. He realized that his body didn't hurt. He tried to sense his body. He circled his neck. It didn't hurt and it didn't feel tight. His shoulder muscles, which usually ached, didn't. He took his hands and massaged his legs, and they seemed less flaccid. His eyes began to adjust to the light. He lifted his arms up and looked at his hands. They were steady. Perhaps a little weak, but they no longer shook. He called out for the dogs and for Min, but no one came or answered.

He leaned back against the headboard and thought for a minute. He didn't hear the rain, which would have explained the power outage. But he did hear the wind, and it was blowing hard. He kicked away at the bed covers and was amazed that he could. He slowly made his way to the edge of the bed and put his feet on the floor. His head was a little dizzy but not much more than that. His eyes kept adjusting to the light, and his body was strong enough to get up.

Stepping over the dog toys, he headed down the hallway, and he realized it might be much later than he thought; he had been sleeping for so long. As he made his way through the house, he saw moonlight come through the windows and glass doors, and he began to see easily. A slight draft touched him and he shivered. Then stepping into the kitchen, he got a glass and filled it with water. He sat at the table, reassured by the newspaper and paperwork still there from breakfast. He drank the water slowly. He didn't know where Min was, but sometimes she would take the dogs and visit her friends down the road. Her friends were chatty and loud and had dogs of their own, and he thought it was good for her. Since he had gotten sick, the house was sometimes too quiet. He often slept for hours, and it was good for her to have noise and motion around her rather than be somewhere where sleep was everything.

Still, it was blowing heavily outside, and she didn't like to drive, especially at night. *Eva.* He suddenly remembered that she was there too. But about Eva, he was less worried. She had lived on her own for years and went wherever she went freely; he thought it was good for her too that she had been out. Even though she had been bright and made jokes, he knew that his illness weighed on her. He wanted so much for her to be happy and for himself and Min to be happy again. He sat in the moonlight sipping his water. His body, at this moment, felt good. He sat in that feeling, moved and grateful. He thought of calling them both but decided it was better for them to be out, and he didn't want to worry them. Too, he was surprised at not hurting, but he didn't want to tell anyone yet; he didn't want to disappoint them if this were momentary.

He stretched and drank more water. The moonlight lay in strips over him. He thought of his twenties, when he had been part of the bon dance group. On August nights he would raise the wooden sticks and hit the taiko drum as people danced in a circle, and he would dance with them too, in a dark blue yukata, with the white cotton hachimaki tied on his head. That pulse ran through him again, strong, and certain, moving in a circle beneath a full moon.

He laughed and thought again of calling them, but then he decided to hold onto this moment, even if just for himself. He stood up and opened the kitchen window. The ginger was blooming, and even on the hardest days, if he could walk out, he would clip stalks to keep in the house. Tonight, there was so much ginger blooming that when he opened the jalousies, the scent flowed through the house, and he breathed in deeply, smiling in a way that he hadn't smiled for months.

After a few more moments in the kitchen, he lifted his arms upward widely and stretched. He put the glass into sink, tired, but a good tired, as if he had made his way up a mountain and back, and now he had earned a good, clean sleep. He walked down the hallway and the slats of light from the moon crisscrossed his path back to the bedroom. He walked into the bathroom and turned on the shower. It was still hot, so the electricity had not been out for long. He pulled off the damp t-shirt, sweats, and socks, and marveled at how easy balance felt; he didn't feel he had to hold onto the bars they had put in the shower or steady himself against the walls. The shower was hot and the steam rose, and the moonlight streamed into his shower, urging his muscles to come alive again. He leaned against the wall to steady himself. It was as if plates of metal had begun to drop off in sheets. Years of thinking, navigating, planning, worrying, and trying to head obstacles off—the weight of carrying so many people in these cases through these years—slid off of him. He took in a breath as if suddenly exposed, as if all these burdens had become him and without them, he wasn't sure what was left. Fear sprang up, but then his soul and his skin continued to breathe. He stood in the shower and let it run all off him, and his soul flooded through his body in ways that it hadn't in a long, long time. The steam rose up from the heat of the water as everything became white and diffused, and he stood as if in the clouds.

He turned off the water and stood. He reached for a thick, heavy towel, and began rubbing his skin dry. His hair still damp, he pulled on clean clothing and stretched out onto the bed. He looked at the ceiling, and he thought of everything he wanted to do. Yet he also realized that he just wanted to lie there and feel his body. He wanted to feel the lack of pain and to breathe long, open, breaths. He promised never to forget this moment and never to take such simple things for granted. He began to feel sleepy, but he wanted to be sure that he remembered everything about this, and in the morning, he would find a way to tell Eva and Min. How, he didn't know, but he might not need to. They might see it in his face—the way he'd walk down the hall—the way he'd wrestle with the dogs—the way he'd reach out to them. Without telling them, they would know.

CHAPTER 9

SLEEP IN HEAVENLY SLEEP

"Sleep," said the man who had found her beneath the trees, away from the shore, "has layers." Eva just sat and listened. He had placed food in front of her, and she was grateful.

He was muscular and wiry. His clothes were simple, well worn, but he was energetic, and quick. She couldn't really tell where he was from or his age. After leaving Lia in the cave, Eva had walked back up from the shore toward the thick rows of trees and had lain down to rest. He had come across her, curled up at the base of the banyans. He had roused her, then led her back inland, swiftly through more trees to another small clearing. There were two small cottages that were built in a small grove; between the cottages was a narrow vegetable garden. In no time, he'd settled her in the cottage on the right that was nearest the trees and taken her to the other where he lived.

When he first found her, he introduced himself as Null. Startled, she could only say, "I'm Eva." He looked at her for a moment, and said, "Yes, it's Null. Null as in zero, nil."

Now she sat at his table and ate the simple food he gave her, listening as he talked. "People have all kinds of experiences," he went on, " or sometimes they're just out. Nothing. Blank. No memory of anything. It all depends."

He collected her plate and put it in the sink. "Sorry I had to rush you. Even now there's no real time for questions,"

When he found her, she had asked him about what he knew, who he was, and how he could help Gene. He said very little. At the time, all he would say was that he would help her find what she needed.

"Time for us all to fall back into sleep," he said, gesturing her to the door after she had eaten. "I'll walk you back."

He walked her in the dark, and she was grateful for the company and the light he carried. His light swung back and forth, and the clouds blocked the moon. The ground was uneven, and the distance between the two cottages seemed farther apart than they had been in the day. He saw her into the cottage, left her his light, and said he could make his way, even in the dark. They said their goodnights, and she began to look around in her cottage. She started to feel cold and looked through the clothing that she found in a narrow closet. She pulled on a thick sweater and something flannel to sleep in. They didn't fit well, but they were clean. She thought about the robe the hosts had given for Gene, and she thought about him, wrapped in it and sleeping. Null was right, she thought, about sleep. She sank through its layers, wanting to sink as quickly as she could.

The next morning, she hurried out of bed. It seemed late, but she took her time in the tiny shower. The narrow vanity had travel-sized toothpaste, toothbrush, and bath soap. *It* is *a guest cottage*, she thought and wanted to laugh. She was happy to feel clean again. She had slept very, very deeply, more than she had in months, and when morning came, she sprang up, eager for the day. She smelled the air and it was so clean, and the air so fragrant. She had never slept in a peace that was as sweet as that.

She packed a few things, including extra socks that had been in a drawer into a small rucksack she found on the floor of the closet. She pulled back her hair and felt awake and clear, as if she had rested for weeks. She ran her fingers over the lotuses on the cuff. She thought of Gene and Min and even of the two dogs and her heart lifted. She thought of the cloak, the mesh of armor; thinking about these things strengthened her.

She made her way to Null's cottage. She was hungry and she hoped he was awake. She had no clock, but it wasn't early.

She knocked, and Null answered quickly. He gestured for her to sit at the table. She saw eggs, oatmeal, and fruit. She smiled and sat down. He had already eaten and was cleaning the pans. She saw his bed was made and a knapsack packed. He turned and saw her eyes on the pack. He said, "I'll be going with you part way. Need to." He continued scrubbing the pans while she ate. "How did you sleep?"

She was chewing and didn't answer at first but eventually said, "Well." As soon as she finished, he took the plates and cleaned them.

"We need to get going," he said and smiled at her. "Bring it," he said, gesturing to the torch, which she had removed from her pack and left on the table. She looked more closely at him and thought he was older than she thought initially. Maybe in his forties or fifties she thought. He was straightforward but cordial, and not a time waster. She nodded, slipped the torch back into her pack and was ready to go. She wanted to ask him more questions, but she didn't, and he didn't offer her any information. Null was already many steps ahead.

claim the ground you walk on

as if the path were birthed for you

They walked without speaking for a good forty minutes to an hour, and she kept up as well as she could. He was taller than she was, and he was faster. He knew where he was going and how to walk between the roots hanging from the banyans and the rocks. She got into a rhythm of following exactly where he stepped and how. It was a choreography of steps, and moving as he did allowed her to follow without thinking. They went up slight inclines and declines, but there was very little to view because the banyans had grown so closely together. The landscape wasn't native, but a strange mix of banyan and bamboo that she had never seen together like this. Unlike Hilo, the air was dry and, in some spots, dusty. In areas that had clearings, the soil itself had swathes of hardened lava flow, which curved around older, mature boulders that were the color of butter. She'd only seen stone like that in in Italy. She had seen an entire city that had been built out of buttered stone, and there, artisans sold glass and ceramics in shops as tiny as cubicles. There she had walked over the yellow cobblestones while the smell of lamb stew drifted in the air.

But here, in this moment, she couldn't tell how near or far they were from a body of water. They stopped several times to drink or eat what he'd carried for them both. She was grateful for that; being with him started to feel familiar and steady. For a moment she recalled the creatures and the pool, and although she hadn't thought of it at that time, she realized it was a lot to go through alone. It was only now, when she wasn't alone, that it started to sink in.

He was quiet and easy and patient when her energy started to flag, but she began to fall farther and farther behind. It was near sunset when they stopped. He didn't explain where they were, and she didn't ask. Speaking and asking seemed clumsy. Just sensing things felt easier.

He had carried blankets for them both, and he gave her one. They sat on them and ate a little, but she was tired and not hungry. The moon rose and it was quiet. The air was cool, but not cold, and she thought of the blue robe and sensed it wrap around her. She heard Null settle down several feet away from her. She looked at the moon, and suddenly missed Gene and Min and home, even California, very much. But then she breathed in deeply and glanced at Null settling into his bedding, and that drew such a sense of peace into her. She felt no mission other than to be there beneath the trees with the light falling between the branches.

She wondered what thoughts Null might have, but his energy was so light that she couldn't feel if he were awake or asleep, and she knew she had to be strong tomorrow. She thanked everything around her, sent love in her heart to Gene, and trusted that she would wake tomorrow and do well.

CHAPTER 10

NULL

At first Null had said no to the powers that be. "Can't take another mission," he said. "I've done my part, given my all. No more to give in that direction." "Time to give others a chance," and he had nodded respectfully to the hosts. He also knew it was his time to rest. All of them were given time, those who had run many missions. And it wasn't about which missions were successful and which ones weren't. It was that there were so many. So many needed help and so many ended up with big clean ups. And it was impossible these days to anticipate what it would take. Anyway, it was sanctuary time for him, and he knew it. It was time, and that's what they allowed the warriors who had been in the field so long. They could rest, study, get away, heal up, and just have space. Some never took up another round of missions after that. Some ascended after sanctuary. Some remained in sanctuary to help the warriors to transition. Some just opted to remain forever in sanctuary after that. That was considered fine too. The light that warriors generated from sanctuary alone was powerful. In fact, some said more powerful. It was centered light; a light that didn't get diluted, and the warriors stayed planted instead of moving from spot to spot like they did on their missions. So when the hosts greeted him at the end of his last mission, he stood, completely at ease. It would finally mark the start of the sanctuary phase for him. They knew it, he knew it, and he needed it. He really, really needed it. He wanted to feel light on his body, in his head and in his heart; he wanted relief from what he had seen for the past years. How many years, he didn't know and didn't want to know. The scars couldn't be seen on his body, but he had them;

he'd also bruised parts of his soul and his own good intentions, and while he was embedded with good, he was exhausted. He was weary, and he had been in such grief when he had seen what had happened to his brother and sister warriors. Many had fallen too, and were in healing and in sanctuary, or in more severe cases, in stasis until they could be revived. Battles had been unexpectedly severe, and for some, it had shaken them, shaken them deeply. They needed to have healing light on them and to soak in pools of light, sometimes for days, weeks, sometimes, he wondered, for their lifetimes. They had performed in noble battles and they had been victorious, but these were difficult times, and their psyches and hearts were injured. Recovering from that required being away and being left in light undisturbed.

So Null had been surprised when the hosts had persisted. He had been quiet as they showed him the vision that they had, when they showed what Eva had shown them days before. They shared the film of her life and of Gene's, and what they had seen in her heart, and the tone of her heart when she had driven up the road and wanted her brother to live.

But the hosts themselves were surprised when Null, clearly moved by what he saw, paused. There was a catch in his voice when he said, "I don't know if I can do it." This, they were not expecting. It caused a hush in the hall, and the hosts were quiet.

There was a long silence. They then focused on Null, on him alone. They looked deeply and saw the layers of him, his goodness, and how the battles had seeped into him, despite all. They also saw the grieving that had stuck to him about the warriors he had lost and now had been separated from him. They saw the uneven results of the last few years and how that had gotten to him. They were silent out of respect and out of appreciation for all that he had done.

"If you could do it, would you?" they asked.

Null sat for a long time. He didn't take this lightly. He had always been a warrior. That was his way. He had been made for this. At the same time, he had begun to feel things slip away from him. Witnessing the suffering of others that had begun to wear at him, especially of the young, the innocent. Although he gave his all, some battles were lost; it was not his place to judge what should or should not have occurred, but the repetition of battle was something he was ready to step away from.

It had begun to sink itself into his bones. He was afraid he wouldn't be able to manage his emotions as well as he always had or even physically move as quickly or to be as resilient. There were times that grief had begun to grip him. Once at the end of a particularly dark battle, the rescuing of children had failed, and their suffering had struck him to the core, and when it had ended, he had fallen, weeping. The ancient books have said when a soul departs earth, all of nature cries out, and at that dark time, he had cried out for all of them.

His elders later explained it was his love for all beings that was transforming him, and if the elders had not intervened at that moment, he would have lost all physical form, but it was not yet his time. They said that sanctuary would eventually bring him peace and that all warriors transform. They acknowledged that he needed to recover to be able to shake this off. The visions of war had begun to seep into his dreams and sleep, and he had begun to think of sanctuary with purpose and longing. Transitions were not easy, and this was one.

The hosts saw all of this. When Null answered finally, "Yes, if I could do this, I would." His eyes were full. His heart was full, yet he was starting to feel broken. He was a warrior who could not fulfill his duty because he had spent all that he had. He was filled with grief for all he could no longer do.

There was silence in the hall, and the hosts bowed their heads. From each of them, there came, at first, a small blue flame, as small as a tear falling from the eyes of a loved one, but the blue flame slowly grew into a deep royal blue that started to flow from all the hosts, to each other, and then down the two levels of tiers, then down toward Null, who had fallen, kneeling. Null was on his knees, his head bowed, and the blue light flowed toward him, over his head, shoulders, torso, and legs. The light stayed over him and then seeped into him and then throughout him, and he began sobbing with grief for all that he had seen and for all that had suffered, and too, for all that he had rescued and served throughout his lifetime as a soul.

The great hall was now filled with blue light, and the hosts and Null remained in this state. There was no sense of time. Gradually, the blue light seeped into all of them until the blue turned into white. The intensity burned through Null, burned through his muscles, his heart, his core, his mind, and all the memories of all that he held before. It blew off all of the darkness that had remained in him, and all of the exhaustion he had accumulated; it turned to ash all that had tied him to his regret, shame, and fear of failing to live up to his duty, and immolated all the wrong he had ever done, rashly, recklessly, thoughtlessly.

Shattered, he remained kneeling. A robed being of light rose above him and showered him with rose-colored light that bathed him like water. He sat, head still bowed, and he wept; he wept this time for joy, for all that had been broken off of him, and all that he knew that lay ahead of him. He knew that this would be the last task before sanctuary, but he had been renewed so that he could do what needed to be done. For that, he was steeped in utter gratitude and humility in the face of forgiving love.

Eva did not know any of this. She knew him only as a quiet Null, who was dressed, fed, and waiting for her to rise.

She woke, feeling strong that morning, and grew stronger still as they walked through the trees. In spots where there was bamboo, the hollow trunks knocked against each other. Where there were banyans, their canopies spread like arms out above them, and when she walked, she looked upwards at the light falling between the spaces of the leaves.

So much of life was beyond what she could do, but today she followed Null more confidently. She let herself observe what surrounded them as they made their way through the trees. The weather grew warmer, but the old banyans shaded them like giant lace parasols, and she smiled to herself as she found the Null's rhythm as picked his way over the roots, fallen branches and patches of wild grass. As she walked, the grass would brush against her legs, and the fragrance of the greens drifted up as the wind moved. Null began to pick up the pace when he saw Eva could keep up. They started to make good time, and Eva focused less on the surroundings and more on keeping pace with Null. Her breath began to quicken as they began to go higher.

"I think I'm doing well," she said, when they took a break for water.

"Didn't say you weren't," Null said, sipping from a flask from his side. She smiled but her brow was a little furrowed.

"Think it's far?" She said looking down at her worn shoes.

"Will knowing that help?" he asked.

She laughed, "No."

"So no point in saying then," he said, and they started up again.

That was the range of their conversation whenever they stopped for water or to eat. But Eva moved on, contented. There was certainty and economy in the way Null carried himself and led the way. She thought of Gene often, but she sensed she was getting closer to something important and that made her feel at ease.

Toward the end of the second day, they reached a plateau. Her muscles ached, but Eva hurried to see what she could see from this height. As Null set up their small camp, Eva stood shivering, because it had started to cool. She looked over the banyans and saw gentle slopes below them. She turned to smile at Null, but he had his back to her. He turned, surveying the direction from where they had come. When he did face her, she smiled, but his look was serious. "We'll need sleep before tomorrow," he said. He gave her a small smile, but then looked toward the direction of the valley. "Any sleep will be good," he said. He had said so little since the first night at the cottage.

The next morning, they both woke early, and they ate and packed quickly. Eva tried to read him, but she could never place what he might be feeling and that worried her.

Null stood and said, "We'll have to move. We need to make quick time to get there before dark."

"Where?" she asked, hurrying, but he didn't answer.

She remembered that he'd said he would go partway with her. She didn't want to know if that part was over soon. She had grown used to his company, and he was easy to be with. She didn't worry about Gene when she was with Null, and they didn't seem to have questions for each other.

They were going downhill now, and Eva realized how slowly Null had paced the previous days for her. He was now at full bore and allowed longer gaps of distance between them, forcing her to keep pace. He was agile, sometimes half leaping down between the roots and rocks, nearly sliding down sections if at sharp declines. After an hour, he took part of what she carried in her pack so that she could move faster.

claim the ground

as if it speaks to you

as sure as the rich earth

delivers spring

Toward the early afternoon, the trees began to thin out and once again, there were strange patches of black lava rock and yellowish sandy soil. Null was far ahead. He waited for her at the edge of grove before it opened into a wide path. When she caught up, he drew her aside, and they stood. He removed her things from his pack, and said, "Okay, Eva," which caught her off guard. He had said her name so rarely. "This is where I stop." He turned her around and removed her pack. She couldn't see his face and didn't say anything.

When she was able to look at him, she said, "Where are we?"

He said, "You haven't gotten where you need to go, but this is where I need to be. You'll be fine. There are others in the next place. They'll help you."

Eva looked at him. Her eyes tried to connect with his. "I'm not leaving you," he said. He seemed to read her, but she could never read him. He had slipped off his pack and was transferring items from his to hers. "I'm still helping you, but from where I am here. I'll always help you."

"Wait." She said, confused. This was the first time that she was so unsure.

"I'm good on my own," she said, looking at him. "But this has worked too," she said, waiting for him to speak.

He was quiet and kept reorganizing his pack and hers.

"I'll do better," she said. "Come with me."

"You're doing fine," he told her, "You've just got a few more things to do." He didn't look at her as he slipped a flask from his pack to hers.

94

"I'll do better if you come with me. Faster." She hesitated, looking at him, "I don't know what I'm doing. I can't mess up."

"You're ready," he said.

"I don't feel ready," she said, looking at him.

"Few do," he said, then smiled at her.

They stood for a few moments, both silent.

After a few moments, looking down, she glanced up at him.

"Thank you, Null."

He nodded, lifting her pack back onto her shoulders, helping to adjust the straps.

When he was done, she turned to look at him, and she nodded.

"Guess it's always inevitable," she said, then turned to walk out of the last section of trees into the open path.

She resisted the desire to look back at him, but after a time she did, and he stood, watching her go. She raised her hand to wave, but she wanted to cry, so she dropped her hand, turned, and started walking faster. She knew she was here for Gene, but now she knew she was here for herself too. What she was doing was sinking into her, deeper than she had realized, and she stepped forward, unsteady, but she kept walking. She wanted to get there before dark.

CHAPTER 11

TIMING

Without Null to pace her, she didn't know if she was slowing, keeping pace, or accelerating. She started to feel agitated. *I get myself into these things. I never know how to get out. I want out.* How far away was she from the hosts, Null, or anything she knew?

She picked up the pace, but the declines were steep, and she was skidding too much. She'd slow but then would try to gauge what time she had. Finally, she had to just settle into whatever she could do. She was now on a wider path, heading away from the plateau with few trees and no shade. There was a sharp decline as the path narrowed, leading her toward a valley. The road kept weaving back and forth with increasingly sharper turns, and after a couple of hours, she started to see patches of green again, a pocket of a valley tucked away. She picked up her pace, and like Null had shown her, nearly running and sliding down the last twisting section that narrowed into a one-man path. She was tired, but her blood pumped with her speed. She was getting closer.

Finally, she made the last curve, and she stood before a small shaded grove, again, with simple cottages, but here there were six. Four to the left, and two set further to the right. Smoke was coming out of the chimneys of the two on the right.

She hesitated. Dust covered her. But she pushed herself to make her way to one of the cottages, walking and dusting herself as she neared. A few feet away from them, she saw one of the doors open, and a woman was inside. She had a tight, narrow face and short reddish-black hair, and she waved for her to come in. Eva smiled, but the woman quickly ducked back into the cottage.

As she neared the doorway, Eva slowed her pace. She began to notice the low grass surrounding the cottages, and the plots had vegetables, but they seemed a bit overgrown, not kempt like Null's. Next to the plot there was a small chicken coop. She could hear the clucking and without realizing it, put her hand on her stomach, as if suddenly remembering the last meal she had with Null.

The doorway was open, and Eva stood waiting. "Come in," the woman said, drying her hands on a towel. "I'm Nora." She smiled, but her eyes studied Eva carefully. Nora turned and started working at the sink, rinsing tomatoes and greens.

"I'm Eva."

"Yes, I know," Nora said, motioning her to sit.

Eva thought of asking about Null, and how Nora knew him, but embarrassment stopped her and said nothing. She also wanted to ask about Gene, but she decided to wait. Instead she said, "If I could clean up ..."

"Sure, through there," and Nora motioned to the small bathroom; the cottage was identical to the one Eva had just stayed in with Null.

Eva slid the pack she was carrying and set it under the table Nora had set. She then closed the door, while Nora continued to prepare a cold meal for Eva.

"I got some of the dust off of me," Eva said when she returned.

"No shortage of that here," Nora said, sliding the vegetables next to the chicken and hot grain she had made for Eva. She glanced quickly as Eva reached for the plate, and a flash of the lotus bracelet slid out from her sleeve. Nora smiled, saying, "Pretty."

Eva smiled back and started to ask a question, but Nora was already leaving.

"I'll be outside if you need me," she said and left Eva to eat.

Eva chewed slowly, taking in the cottage. It was homey and spare, identical to Null's. She was hungry and thirsty, and the food was good. Her bones and muscles were suddenly aware of the climbing and walking she had done in the past days. She put the dishes in the sink, washed them, picked up her pack, and went out the door.

"You can take the cottage at the very end," Nora said, not looking up from the garden patch that she was weeding. "We'll talk in the morning."

Eva hesitated. She wanted to say something, but Nora continued to work her hands in the earth.

Eva looked up. It was beginning to get dark, and she was glad she had nearly sprinted the last few rounds on the path to get here when there was light.

Back in her cottage, she took a long hot shower and helped herself to the fresh clothing in the drawers. This time there was a soft, thick sweater that was blue, and she slid it over her head and slipped into the bed. As she began to fall asleep, she wondered if she would see Null again.

But only after an hour or two, a rumble woke her. The whole room shook, and the cups on the shelves rattled. A couple of them slid off and shattered. Seconds passed, but a bigger rumble started. She slipped on her shoes and ran outside.

Two women were standing outside in the dark, and the shapes of their bodies and faces moved in the moonlight. "Eva!"

"Nora!" Eva called and ran over to them.

The earth kept moving, enough to make the three drop to the ground; they were now in the center of the small grove, away from trees and houses. Chickens squawked in distress, and she heard a dog barking nearby. The earth gave another extended long shake, and then it stopped.

They lay there in the dark for a few seconds. They were waiting for the aftershocks, which came in quick succession. It reminded Eva of the few months she had lived in Northern California and then Alaska; she became accustomed to the rumbling and the sliding, the breaking dishes. But these quakes were deeper and coming in longer waves.

Gradually, they began to sit up, and Nora tried to see in the dark.

"This is Raila," Nora said. The woman, an elder, had long, braided hair, but Eva couldn't see much beyond that. The elder moved carefully, and her arm rested on Nora's.

Nora gestured for Eva to follow, and the three started to walk back to the cottages.

#

101

Eva had learned about darkness. It scared her, the things she had seen. People would walk down corridors or a quiet city street, and in an unfortunate moment, darkness might latch onto them. Needles and thorn-like prongs might attach themselves to a human's spine, or creatures might scamper alongside humans only to pounce on them and cling, suddenly inducing their human carriers to snarl at whatever might walk by. The souls who carried these beasts on their backs were good and decent; the creatures that clung on their backs were not.

Eva knew she was finally becoming awake. That's why she could see the things she could see. It made things harder and it made them easier. She knew where the lines were drawn. The worst was when she lied to herself, trying to tell herself it wasn't as bad as it was, or that she didn't see what she did. Only light would calm her down. She'd close her eyes and go inward and ask for that light to spill outward. That worked, and on other days, the only thing she could do was circumnavigate, keep above the fray, or on bad days, just run.

CHAPTER 12

ALL THAT IS MALLEABLE

Eva lay on the cot, burning up.

Raila, the elder, was worried. "We can't let them get her."

Nora sat and moved her hand through her short hair. "But I'm tired of losing," she said. "I'm tired of war."

"You're too young to be tired. And what about me," asked Raila, "do I have a right to be tired?" She sat, tapping the table. Her eyes were cloudy. She raised her hand to feel the round silver disk on the long leather strand that hung around her neck.

"No. None of us has the right." Nora got up from the table, picking up some of the pieces of broken cups shattered by the quake, throwing them into a basket. Her hair was thick and seemed to bristle as she spoke.

Raila reached out and tugged at Nora's arm, "Don't forget. You are my eyes." Nora jerked back, dropping the fragments she'd lifted from the floor.

"We are bound," she continued, "in the best of ways."

Nora twisted her arm to get out of her grasp. "I don't forget," Nora said.

Raila laughed, and said, "Don't take things personally."

"You wouldn't have it any other way," Nora replied, running her hands over her scalp. "She'll sleep," Nora said, looking at Eva lying on the cottage bed. She knelt to pick up the last fragments of the broken cups.

Raila was quiet. She stood up as Nora moved toward the door.

"In the morning, then," she said, grasping Nora's arm to steady herself and to be led out. She kept walking as Eva twisted in the bed. "She's not going anywhere tonight."

#

Null was agitated. He knew he had to remain where he was, but he struggled against it. He hadn't thought well of the plan to begin with. He had argued with the others that he should go with Eva. She had been making good time with him pacing her. But he knew that there was a reason for her to go alone though he didn't know what it was. He didn't like it, but he would have to wait; he could pack, but he would wait to be sure. If he had to, he could go after her.

#

In the world Eva knew now, all things were malleable. Earth, tree, water. Everything was merging and liquid. Her body sank, heavy. Exhausted, she kept going deeper into the liquid that received her, and she began to submerge, pulled into the thickness, into the viscous water.

I feel the urgency of time
but I still find my way to the ocean
it lies before me
a bright blue piece of glass
holding in a yellow heat
turning into photosynthesis green

#

At the house, Gene was sleeping lightly. In this state, he started to see beautiful translucent jewel colors of dyed silk. The silk pieces moved and fluttered as if they were in a giant sky. They rippled like the languid tails of goldfish, and he nearly laughed at their elegance. His chest expanded and he breathed deeply; submerged, it was as if he belonged under water, as if he belonged in this world. His senses were alive and clear. He kept sinking further and further, and his body took to it. He took to it as if he were made of the sea himself and began to kick and dive far below the water's surface, with a joy he hadn't had in years.

He swam past vivid, living coral beds of all shades of color and hue. He saw silver, yellow, blue, black fish swimming between rays of light. He dove past them and circled back, swimming with them for great lengths. He saw the turtles and reached out to touch an old one's shell, and the turtle looked at him with one long blink and then it returned to the sea grass beds.

He kicked his legs, and his clothing was nearly translucent, like the silk he had seen. He was muscled and lithe, and his arms and legs were strong as he pulled through the water. He needed no air, without any pressure to return to the surface.

But then as he swam, he experienced a vague pull. The remembrance of something. He paused for a moment, curving his body, and he was filled with sorrow and freedom. He held there for a moment, suspended. Then he slowly began a vertical ascent upwards, kicking his legs, arms by his side, letting himself swim upwards gradually to break to the surface.

To his left, he began to see the fuzzy outline of a woman swimming toward him.

When he woke, it was morning. The dogs were back and lying next to him. So was Min. She was already getting up and calling the dogs. He didn't want to speak yet or move. He kept his eyes closed and let her leave the room with the dogs.

He lay there, afraid to know the state of his body.

CHAPTER 13

THE TREES

Eva woke up in the cottage with a start, coughing and wanting to spit out something bitter. It was dark. "Quiet," a terse voice said to her, and a hand clasped over her mouth. When she opened her eyes in the dark, she saw it was Null, his face close to hers. He shook his head, *no*. His hand was over her mouth, and he had her in a firm grip, his forearm pinning her. He waited a few seconds. Her fear turned to anger, and she tried to pull away, but he was immovable. She closed her eyes and let herself feel what he felt. Her heart slowed. She let the tension out of her body. She opened her eyes. He looked at her, and she tried to nod her head.

He let her go. She breathed. She knew now how much strength Null had and how quickly he could change. He was unflinching when she had struggled. Nothing had moved him.

It was dark in the cottage, and she let her eyes adjust. Her head hurt and she was groggy. She remembered the quake but not much else.

"We need to leave," he whispered, motioning for her to pick up her bag.

When Eva looked at him, asking, "But what about them?"

"They'll be taken care of," he said, as Eva continued waiting, looking at him for an answer. "They'll turn on themselves," he said, "like they always do." He pulled the handle on the large kitchen window of the cottage, and cool air rushed in. The grove of trees lay behind the cottage.

"I don't understand," Eva said. She reached her hand out to steady herself against a chair.

"Hurry," Null said.

113

Eva threw on her shoes and grabbed her pack. While Null was sliding his pack on, she reached out for the small container of grain she'd left on the counter from dinner, but Null grabbed her arm and shook his head. Startled, Eva looked at him. It had been the last thing she had eaten before going to bed and before the quake. Nora had prepared it for her.

They slid out of the window; first Null, then Eva, and they took off. The chickens were the only ones who heard them, and they were preoccupied with keeping the eggs under them warm.

The two half jogged, half sprinted. Null took the lead, and he wove in between the trees and the roots, with Eva following him. He moved with ease, and Eva quickly threw her pack to him so that she could keep up. There was little light from the moon, but when it fell, it marked them in slivers and triangles of light.

She had left the cottage feeling sick and dulled, but when Null set the pace, whatever she had in her was being sweat out of her skin, and he became easier to follow. She knew they were running away, but she was buoyed by an odd exhilaration and companionship. It was strange, but she smiled, and her body began to relax. The sound of their steps hit the ground, steady and rhythmical as they twisted their way through the trees. Right now, she didn't want to think but just wanted to move as he did. He didn't look back toward her. He could hear her replicating how he moved, and he kept up their speed. He wanted to move her as quickly as he could from the cottages. Suddenly, anger flickered up in her, but she focused on the sound of Null running ahead. She didn't want to think about the two behind them or the mistakes she may have made with them. She wanted to keep running, to burn out run everything that was wrong with her. The moon left optical illusions of horizontal light on them as they ran, as if they were shadows seen through windows on a train, with the shadows of trees moving with them. The night kept the temperature cool, and as she ran, her legs kept getting lighter and lighter.

It was nearly dawn when Eva noticed Null had begun slowing and tracking. Her muscles were beginning to hurt and she was glad he slowed. She couldn't tell what he was looking for, or why he dropped their speed. There was no grove or clearing, just thick, rooted trees. He also kept looking, not at the ground, but at the branches above. Finally, he slowed and then veered to the right, then circled back. He looked upward, and then settled below one. For the first time, he gave her a half smile, and she sat as ropes descended from the trees.

#

Little Bird, Little Bird, good morning!
Little Bird, Little Bird, good day!
Little Bird, Little Bird, sweet dawning
Little Bird, Little Bird, at play

When Eva woke the next morning, the lyrics were running through her head. Eva remembered her mother and then her brother singing them to her.

Little Bird, Little Bird, come greet me
Little Bird, Little Bird, please stay

Her body started to feel the run they'd had in the night. She turned on her side on the thin padded mattress and stretched her legs out. In the predawn hours, exhausted as she was, she had scaled her tree with its descending ropes, just as Null had his, negotiating her way up the ropes and a narrow-slatted ladder. Now she was forty-plus feet above ground, resting on planks secured by tongue and groove. She had slept deeply despite the sun overhead. The light moved over her as she lay there, spots of heat falling between the branches and the leaves. She thought of Null and wondered if he had woken yet. She shifted and sat up; she moved carefully from the narrow pallet and looked over the railing that was hidden in the leaves. He was already below, talking quietly to two other men making breakfast over the fire. The two looked similar enough to be brothers to Null, but one looked older and the other slightly younger. She felt happy, but then quickly stepped back when she realized how long she had been watching them.

The sun is awake and yawning

115

The moon and stars slip away to hide

Wings unfolding

Then up and away you fly

close his eyes and drift off to Eva slid down the rope to the ground, bypassing the rope ladder, half sliding, half rappelling against the trunk. Null and two other men had finished eating, and Null handed her a plate.

"Eva, this is Jens and Hugo."

Jens, who seemed younger than the two, smiled, and as he did, she noticed a small scar at the side of his lower lip. He handed her a plate with eggs and bread, and Hugo stood up, stretching out both his hands to clasp hers, then gestured for her to sit with them. His hands were warm and calloused, and his eyes were kind. Both men nodded when she said, "Thank you for having me here."

"Glad you made it," Jens said. He handed Eva a fork, then began stacking the other's finished plates.

Hugo looked down and laughed softly. His eyes were bright, and he rubbed his hand through the stubble on his chin. "Heard you almost didn't make it." After a pause he said, "That would have been Null *and* Void," and he laughed, as Jens scrubbed a plate in a shallow pan of water.

Null, who was still eating, stiffened.

Eva didn't know what to say. She turned to him, and said, "I thought Nora and Raila were your friends."

The three men were quiet. Jens kept cleaning, but Hugo spoke, getting up slowly, stretching the stiffness out of his legs.

"They split off from the group a while ago. They're on a different mission now."

Eva looked at Null. He didn't look at her and handed his plate to Jens.

"To do what?" Eva said.

Jens hesitated, but then started to put out the fire. He kept working and said nothing.

Hugo looked at Jens, then at Null.

The three men were silent.

#

Jens and Hugo were now like brothers even though it began with some tension. Jens was more of an observer in those early days. Hugo tended to play on that, treating Jens like a younger brother, goading him at times. Hugo was a bear of a personality. Nothing was timid. His laughter, his challenges to authority, his questions sometimes tested others' patience.

This did not sit well with Jens when he first joined the group of Null, Hugo, Nora, and Raila. He came late to their cycle of training, unsure of what role he would play. If given a choice, he would have worked in solitude, to be alone on his missions. But the needs of others came first, and he chose to accept when the opportunity arrived.

He had expected an atmosphere of quiet and discipline. Instead, there was a sense of informality and surprise, which suited Hugo, who was open to the point of being brash.

"I'd love to know what goes on in that mind," Hugo said, gesturing to Jens as they moved down a trail.

"If you said less," Null told Hugo. "you might find out."
Hugo laughed, and Null gave a quick nod to Jens.

Jens gave little expression but was grateful to Null. As the newest to join, he felt he was in over his head, and he didn't realize it until much later that they all felt the same.

The day after Jens arrived, the group met in soft morning light to learn remedies from the botanist. They had to trek a distance into a narrow valley. Recent wildfires had blackened the hillsides nearby, and they had to expand to new areas to forage for what they needed.

As they entered the valley floor, Jens was attentive but chose to fall to the back. He felt easily distracted, and following the others helped him keep focus. The air was cool and damp, and the botanist's voice was steady and quiet. Jens wanted to the sounds of the trees and air, without having to hold onto words, but pushed himself to think and keep up with the group.

"So what do you think?" Hugo asked Null, gesturing to Jens, when the group reached a small clearing and gathered around the botanist.

The two stood quietly talking, away from the others.

"I see potential," Null said, turning toward Hugo.

"Inexperience," Hugo said. He paused and continued, "and a little uncertainty."

"That's a sign of humility. Not a bad thing," Null responded.

"Depends on the cause. Unsure about himself... or us?" Hugo said.

The two men joined the others as the botanist pointed out the lichen on the branches of the trees.

Jens listened but then crouched down to run his hands through the soil. Hugo had moved closer to listen to the botanist, who believed in knowing formulas by heart, not by notation.

Null was concentrating as well, trying to memorize as they went. Raila and Nora were quiet, with Raila leaning on Nora.

When the group clustered around the lichen to study more closely, Jens made his way to Null. "Noticed something?"

Null looked for a moment away from the base of the tree. "What do you mean?"

"The texture. Or mixture." Jens kneeled down, grabbing a handful of the soil. "Silt." He looked up at Null, pointing to moist rivulets of fine mud running down a slope near them. "But only in spots."

Hugo was out of earshot, helping Nora tend to Raila, who was following the botanist as he moved to another tree.

"Tell Hugo," Null answered, gesturing in their direction.

Jens looked back at Hugo. "Maybe. Or it might be nothing."

Hours later, the botanist, the eldest, was tired, and wanted to head back. They kept their respective positions so Jens, who had been last, was now—uncomfortably—head of the pack. Everyone followed, with the botanist last.

There was fatigue in the air. They were silent and Jens set a steady pace, almost serpentine, as they wrapped their way around the large, rooted trees and old fallen trunks. The air was damp, ideal for the lichen and mosses they were studying. As they made their way, Raila looked at the sky. Hugo nodded as Jens picked up the pace.

Nora wrapped a shawl tighter around herself and pulled up a hood around Raila. The other men looked at each other as the wind increased. It had started to rain.

Jens turned to look back at the men first, then at Raila. Despite her struggling, Jens picked up the pace of the line. Hugo fell back to help the botanist over the roots and tight spaces. Null slowed to help Nora with Raila. Jens moved forward more quickly as the rain hit more

118

rapidly. He noticed the rain as it struck the surfaces around them. Hugo called from the back. He gestured to Jens to keep a straighter, less circuitous path, and Jens nodded. Raila, with the help of Nora and Null, was forced to scramble over the knotted trees to cut time. They no longer avoided the larger, twisted trunks that lay in their way, but instead, scaled them directly.

They were headed down to a small dip into the path and then up again. There were several stretches like that remaining. The sound of the rain increased and so did the wind. Jens felt his skin chill. Images of the blackened hillside, the wildfires, and the strange sediment merged: they were standing on a new flood plain.

He turned sharply and gestured to Hugo that they should head to the left, up a slope to higher ground. He saw that Nora had already realized the same and started to lead Raila diagonally, away from the path they were on. Hugo had also begun leading the botanist in the same direction, turning back to see the increasing pools of water behind them. Null fell back and he and Nora helped Raila regain her footing upward as the slope steepened. The rain increased.

Jens then left the lead to help Hugo and the botanist, who was sliding on the thick roots that were now more exposed by the eroding soil. Hugo was strong enough to help lift the botanist up above the roughest spots, and Jens supported him from the back. Mud began to cover them all as the soil slid beneath their feet. They scrambled up the slope, with heavy silt and chunks of earth melting away below them, the dark earth mixed with broken roots and branches. Soaked and muddied, they were moving as quickly as they could to the left, away from the dipping path toward higher ground.

The rain was pouring, and thunder cracked in intervals. The low slope they were climbing was an increasingly steep wall formed by the shearing off of earth. The ground was growing saturated and dark, and vertical sheets peeled off, sagging beneath their climbing feet as it fell to the narrow valley path below.

Jens left Hugo and the botanist to scramble up to the highest point, turning to pull the others up. Deep roots on the slope were now exposed, and when the climbers could, they used those as footholds and handholds to move up the steep incline. Hugo and the botanist began to gain ground, and Jens pulled them up to where he stood. Raila kept reaching out but sliding back, so Nora and Null placed themselves before and after her, helping her until she neared the top. Nora kept turning back to look at the path as they drew away from it. She could hear the impact of rain and a faint knocking of wood against wood, as behind them, the rain was loosening fallen trunks and branches into moving water.

When Raila finally reached the last way up, they began to hear what sounded like an odd chattering of birds and the approaching sound of water smacking against surfaces, the slaps of mud against rock, the clacking of stone against stone, and a hiss of water moving at rapid speeds. They rallied to make the final push and pull to get Raila to the highest point and away from the falling mud and sludge.

There they lay on the ledge, in exhaustion, as the water melted earthen walls, tumbled trees, and drowned vegetation that had become as limp as sea grass. The rain struck every surface, gathering itself together or splitting itself apart to cover everything it could.

But it was only a moment they lay panting as the rain hit them, their breath frosting in the cold. Jens got up, with Hugo following, pulling Raila and the botanist further away from the sheer wall that continued to be eaten away. They receded yards back, until they were beyond safe, and then they sat until the rain began to subside and the flood eased. They then stood, looking below at the sediment, silt, and battered trees, which filled the path they had walked on that morning.

#

"It's hard to explain how or why things happen," Hugo said, as Eva slept above them in the trees. "As you say, gaps make people learn, figure things out," Hugo said to a tense Null.

"But what falls into that gap?" asked Null. "Interference? Providence?"

"Seen both," Hugo said.

Jens glanced at Hugo.

Hugo went on as Null shook his head. "So what's the alternative? Always knowing? Always in control? No uncertainty?"

"No. But it's a matter of readiness. What are people ready for? And when?" Null answered.

"It's timing," Jens said.

"Or willingness," Hugo added.

The three men looked at each other, thinking of Nora and Raila, as they heard Eva descend from the tree to join them for breakfast.

Nora and Raila had found a way to intervene. Whatever the root cause, it had been timing, as if Eva had gotten on the wrong train and arrived early. The two usually chose to stay on the periphery. The men knew now that had changed, but whatever it had changed to, they needed to keep moving Eva ahead.

"We'll have to sort them out later," Hugo said just as Eva joined them.

The men kept working but were silent as Eva finished her breakfast. "Not a place for direct questions, I guess," she said softly to herself and them.

"When you're finished, we'll have a day trip, but we'll be back," Null said.

She didn't know why they hadn't answered her, but she was tired and relieved to hear she could return to the trees to sleep that night. She had been on the move for days now. She also wanted another night way up above the ground. As stiff as her body was, she had slept deeply, and she had dreamt of the songs of her mother. She even thought of asking if she could stay back, but she thought of Gene. She was tired, but that didn't matter much. She looked at Null and nodded that she was ready to go.

Jens took her plate from her, smiled, refusing her offer of help as he finished cleaning up the site. Hugo rose stiffly, stretching his legs out again, then walked with Null and Eva a few yards from the banyans.

"You want to go north today," and Hugo pointed toward the mountain, handing them their packs "Go as quickly as you can," he said. "Time will be tight so get back before dark." Null nodded, adjusting the pack on his shoulders. He reached out to help Eva with hers, but she quickly secured it herself. "I'm okay," she said a little tersely.

Hugo looked at Null, smiled at them both and said, "Remember the time," then headed back.

Eva hesitated, thinking about the good sleep there was in the trees, but turned and followed Null.

Her muscles were sore, and she couldn't follow him as quickly as she had the previous night. The ground was uneven from the ripples of old and new hardened lava. Too, they were ascending, and Null would have to pause and guide her up certain sections. Out of pride, she kept up as quickly as she could, but sometimes she ignored the directions he gave her. *No answers to my questions*, she thought. She struggled with her legs aching. *What has following gotten me anyway? Earthquakes and passing out?* She thought back to Raila's grayed-out eyes and the look Null gave her when she had tried to bring the grain from the cottage.

She also didn't like these heights or the terrain, which was new and hybrid. The yellowy stacks of rocks were large and needed rigorous scaling. She dreaded the descent on their return, but she couldn't think about it. She thought less about following Null and more about Gene. She couldn't tell for sure, but she sensed he was doing better and in better spirits. They were close that way, and could sense how each other might be, whether they were communicating or not. She hoped she was right.

She started to fall back, however, as the sun rose and the inclines became sharper. She started to skid and slip back in places, and she had scratches and abrasions. The air was dry and it was hot. They took a break before scaling a particularly sheer face. She sat down and leaned against the hot stone; they took long drinks of water.

She felt guilty about her sullenness. "I like your friends," she said, thinking about Jens and Hugo, "even though they don't explain much." Looking at Null, she said, "They're funny." She paused then asked, "Did you grow up together?"

"Trained together. That's what makes us like brothers. Hugo's a good soul. You can learn a lot from him. Jens has. I have."

"Before I thought…" she said.

"I know. Hugo and Jens were supposed to be the ones to meet you there."

Eva turned to look at Null, "So why were the other two there?"

"Hard to explain why people do what they do sometimes." Null's jaw was tight. He stood up. "Let's keep moving," he said.

"But who are they? What happened?"

Null didn't answer and started the next ascent first, moving onto the smaller rocks and then up to the larger boulder. She saw the footholds he took and how he leveraged his weight up quickly. She followed him but she moved too slowly and started to slide. She frowned and slid. Yellow dust began to fly up, which she tried not to breathe. Her skin began to burn from the heat and abrasions from the rocks. He turned to watch her, but she recovered, and he moved ahead. He quickened his pace as they got closer to more level ground.

When they got to the top of the mountain, she saw it was primarily flat, but one section was slightly raised up like a small broken tooth. There were only a few small sections with ground and trees over them. It was a gravely, gritty soil that crunched under their feet.

"Over here," Null said, walking, and despite the rocky soil, he found small patches of green. The heat and lack of tree cover were taking a lot out of Eva. While Eva sat, Null pulled out a small pouch from his back pocket, kneeled, then brushed his hands through what grew. After a few minutes, he held up a leafy looking weed with a purplish blossom, similar to red clover. "This is what we're looking for," he said, and he put it in the pouch.

"For Gene?" Eva asked quickly. She hadn't brought him up since he had taken her to the cottage.

He was quiet for a moment. "It's for you," Null said. "It counters what you got at the cottage."

"What do you mean?" Eva said and stopped reaching for the pouch.

"It helps cut any lasting effect." Null knelt, running his fingers in the earth and green at his feet. "Then we'll get something else for Gene."

Anger shot through her toward him and the strange pair at the cottages. And herself. She wasn't clever or careful. That's how she always got into trouble. She bit her lip thinking of how she had made assumptions. Going to the cottages, trusting those two, and frankly, following Null, Jens, and Hugo. She looked away from Null. She had herself to worry about too, not just Gene.

Null looked up at her. He gazed at her for a moment, then back at the earth. He got up and moved to another patch of green. He moved his fingers through and then put another leaf and blossom into the pouch.

"Start looking," he said.

She looked at him briefly, unsmiling, then knelt next to him. They both began running their hands gently through patches to uncover the wildflowers sprinkled among the green. After an hour, they had filled the small pouch with the blossoms and the leaves.

Null then moved over to the last few trees before the scrub and jagged rocks began. "Here," he called to her, "but take only what you need."

She saw from where she stood that there was deep green ground cover, but instead of purple, there were yellow wildflowers sprinkled through. Null was picking the blossoms, and he held one up to her.

"This," he said.

He pulled two other pouches from his pocket, one for her and one for him. "Hurry," he said, "we've got to get back."

The flowers were delicate, and Null wanted her to preserve the roots if they could, so they had to be careful extracting them from the ground. They didn't talk but swept their way, back and forth through several patches, careful to take what they could, but leaving enough so that the growth could survive.

When both had pouches that were slightly full, they stopped. Null looked at the sky, gauging time, and they started back down the rocks.

Descending was trickier for Eva. She could climb up fairly well but climbing down made her nervous. Null seemed impatient, hurrying her by allowing wide gaps of distance to fall between them. On one cliff face, she paused; she hadn't been close enough to see how he had climbed down, and he turned to look at her, but then kept moving ahead. She tried walking forward, down the smaller rocks, but she started to skid and slip. She had to turn around to face the cliff, find places large enough to grip, and footholds that were big enough. She slid part way, scraping her arm, but she held on, and most importantly, she had swung the pouch to the side so it wouldn't be crushed. She thought of Raila and Nora, and the anger made her pick up her speed. She banged her wrist and the bracelet a couple of times against the rocks, *that's not doing me any good*, she thought, but she didn't stop. *Who cares?* She let herself half slide and half climb down, with small rocks dislodged and scattering, but she had better balance moving faster than slower, and she made it down.

She was mad and anxious. Null was out of sight. She slid down through the areas she could and sprinted on the areas that were more level until she made it far down enough to have Null again in sight. He turned briefly when he heard her coming, but he picked up the pace, and they reached the camp of trees before dark.

Back at the camp, she handed her pouch to Hugo and Null, who were waiting for her, and without a word, she went straight to the ropes to get to her pallet in the trees. Before she headed up, Null handed her a small kit to dab at the scratches, which she stuck into her pack, unsmiling. She didn't see Jens, nor did she care. She was tired, bruised and scratched, and she thought about Gene. She had lost her focus, and she now faced the urgency of time. She grabbed at the rope ladder to go above as they started working on the herbs. She tried to pull herself up, but the pack tipped her too far back and she started dangling beneath the tree. She'd had an easier time the first day. Today she didn't care what they saw or thought about her. She was too tired to worry about it.

Null and Hugo didn't care whether she made it up there either and weren't watching her as she struggled, failing several times. The men were already at work with what they had gathered. She made a couple more attempts, one that had her twisting in the air, and another had her banging into the tree. On a different day she would have laughed and asked for help, but today, she just dangled, spun, got angry, and half kicked and climbed, until she made her way up.

Hugo and Null were focused on the herbs. What Eva's remedy needed was a simple, hardy preparation. They could just rinse the clover-like blossoms, drop them into a worn strainer, and then steep it into a bright violet tea.

Gene's had to be handled more carefully. Water was precious, and they filled a small pot up to an inch or two to clean off the fragile herbs and stems. They had to pick through the blossoms and the tendrils of stems without bruising them. They were two men with calloused hands, manipulating small flowers carefully. Hugo's hands in particular were scarred and thick, so he let Null do most of the delicate work.

It was the botanist who shared everything he knew about the forest and the growing things. He had been a strict taskmaster, and he had to be. Jens had suffered a major wound, chin to cheekbone, but through the benefit of the botanist, had limited scarring to a small, discreet line near his lip. In the same way that they could benefit, errors with preparation could be fatal. The botanist had schooled them on the power of what was in the forest, and it had stuck with them.

After cleaning the blossoms and stems, Hugo and Null took them out and lay them next to a glass bowl. They looked at each other before the next step. They needed to blanch the blossoms and stems very quickly and lightly and then drop them into a small amount of room temperature water to steep. Too much could be toxic to the liver and kidneys, but not enough wouldn't cause any effect, and they would have wasted the herb. The sun was going down and they hurried to make use of the light.

Null dropped the greens and blossoms in the hot water, counted to three, and then scooped them out. He then immediately dropped them in a glass bowl with a several inches of water. After they steeped for several minutes, he removed the stems to reserve them for another remedy. As the blossoms continued steeping, Hugo rummaged through his own pack for a flask. When the liquid in the glass bowl completely cooled, Null poured it through a funnel into the flask and capped it. It was done, and both Null and Hugo exhaled. Null put the flask in a padded pouch and slipped it into a backpack that lay away from the fire.

Jens returned, and while he helped clean up, Hugo stamped out the last embers of the fire completely, and then buried it under earth. He then used a branch to sweep over the ground cover around the circumference of the tree to restore any areas they had flattened with their footsteps or packs. All three men then headed up to the trees themselves. All of them, including Eva, slept deeply that night, and the light from the moon was soft and diffused, allowing them a gentleness they needed.

CHAPTER 14

THE GROVE

When Eva woke the next morning, she saw only Jens, who was packing up what the men had used to cook that morning. He smiled as he handed her a bit of bread and fruit and asked if she had slept well. She nodded and asked about Null and Hugo.

"Null will be back," Jens smiled again, and she saw his eyes were brighter than the first day. He paused as if he might say more, but instead used a pulley to raise the climbing ropes to be hidden among the branches of the trees. He slid on his own pack and said to Eva before he left, "You're doing better than you know. We're all learning."

Eva nodded, watching him until she could no longer see him work his way through the trees. The expression of worry on her face didn't change. She sat and waited. No mark remained of anyone having been there, except the last scent of earth and smoke, the evidence of a fire cooled and buried beneath ground.

She didn't wait long. Soon she heard rustling, and the rhythm of steps she recognized.

Null appeared, smiling, and as he approached, he said, "Hugo's already gone and Jens will join him. They're going to the mountains." He turned to look at her. "We're headed east."

She nodded, giving him a small smile. They slid on their packs, and he led her out at a fast clip. She took a quick moment to turn to look at the trees, but she couldn't tell which trees had been her home, as if they had all clustered together to become indistinguishable to hide where they had been.

Null seemed in good spirits. "Start drinking this," he said, smiling as he moved, and as she moved close behind him, he handed her a narrow flask. The second flask, Gene's, he held on a loop on his hip. When she sipped hers, she saw it was a beautiful violet color. It was sweet, and it quenched her thirst. It made her woozy for a moment, but then fatigue ran off her body. He watched her.

"About the other day—" she started. Her stomach twisted in a knot for a moment then untwisted. She looped the bottle on her hip, and walked faster, but when she turned, Null was already out of range and picking up speed.

They kept a good clip for several hours. Null had hushed her when they started to approach the second grove. The first he had wanted to avoid. He didn't cross through it, but instead had them remain in the thick of the trees, going around the perimeter quickly. Eva had followed him, and he allowed no gap between them, even though she was moving slowly.

"Feeling better?" he asked, turning back to look her.

She nodded but kept her eyes on the ground to keep from stumbling.

The trees were more densely packed, the roots more overgrown, and light from the sky was less. It took her longer to make her way through.

Just when they reached the edge of the trees, just before the grove, he slid off his pack and gestured for her to remove hers.

He found a comfortable trunk to lean against. "We have to wait here," he said, as she took off her pack and sipped from the flask. "We're guests. They are my friends but be careful." Her eyes widened, and recapping the flask carefully, she nodded. "Just take your cues from me—and them," he said.

"Now we wait," he said.

Eva looked at him. "Time's important," she said. "Gene."

"That's not lost on me," Null said, "but I'm not in control of that." He closed his eyes and kept leaning back onto a tree.

"Then who is?" she asked, looking cross.

"Not me," Null said, folding his arms and shutting his eyes.

Drowsy, she settled beneath another tree. They seemed to wait forever. Null didn't seem impatient, but he was hard to read. She started to say something but calmed herself by looking upward.

After an hour or so, Null got up and listened as if he heard something. Eva stood up, and Null gave her a look. "Take your cues from me and them," he repeated, and then he led her into the grove.

Eva was directly behind him, and when he finally stopped, she stepped to his right so that she could see for herself what was ahead.

Rise to the window, "Spring, dear!"
Raise up the curtain now
Breathe in the morning glory
Hear all the birds in song

She heard the singing first. Then she saw over a dozen miniature cottages as small as toys in clusters of four but not in straight rows. Each cottage had a door or window facing east. It was a small clearing, and she saw very tiny beings, very fuzzy, golden, and gauzy in outline. It was a village, and all the beings were at work.

Sing to the rays of sunshine
Dance to the morning dew
Bow to the scent of flowers
All for the love of you

Some had wings that she could see, and some did not. But the music and voices were what she could hear. She also heard a soft whirring sometimes. As they chopped wood, harvested food, repaired their cottages and tended to plants in the ground, she could hear them.

All joy all joy
Ring true through stone
All joy all joy
Let waters flow

All love, all love

Sing anthems high

All love, all love

For spring is here

She turned to Null, and he smiled. "Be careful," he said again. "They are my friends." Null turned toward them, saying, "They warrant the kindest care."

She heard the tenderness in his voice and realized that it was she who needed to show care with them, and it was their vulnerability, not hers, that he had been alerting her to. Embarrassed, she regretted being cross.

Null stepped forward, and she followed. Eva stepped much more delicately among them, and she saw how easily they were affected. Like jellyfish swaying in water, the light beings would fly closer or farther away depending on the nature of her thoughts. Eva gave a quiet smile to Null; he knew she now understood.

The two moved, with the light beings clustering around them, onto a shaded patch of grass. The air hummed, thick with light, and the songs continued. They gathered, creating shining clouds around them, bringing sweets, pitchers of water, fruit, and flowers that they pulled in small carts. The sunlight shined through the glass pitchers and everything glowed like honey. Rays also refracted off the Eva's silver cuff, and she thought of the shiny eyes of the woman at the gallery. Null sat closely to her. They were surrounded by gifts and the light beings. He nodded before them, saying very softly, "dear friends."

Come all ye lovers spring's here

All that a heart employs

Move to the spirit growing

Turn to the earth now poised

Strike up the pose of heroes

Take up a gleeful vow

Promise to love unending
Winter is gone for now

They sang as Eva and Null sat among them. Sometimes the beings flew, and Eva watched them as they circled. They glowed and the hazy gauze took on different shades of color and there was so much fragrance in the air. They brought water bowls and towels so that Null and Eva could wash their hands and cleanse their faces before eating.

All joy, all joy
Ring true through stone
All joy, all joy
Let waters flow

Eva bowed her head. A deep sweetness rose in her chest. She looked at Null.

All love, all love
Sing anthems high
All love, all love
For spring is here

The two sat, flooded by attention.
Null closed his eyes.
When he had first begun his missions, Null had so much to learn. He had always had a fiery temperament and impatience with time. His will and moods made him feel so rough and tumble compared to others who did this work.

After an early mission, he had been sent to this grove to meet with the small light beings, all just two to three inches in size. He didn't know why he was sent to them. They had just begun work to develop the grove. He guessed he was there to give suggestions on their work. There were only three completed cottages, and they had the beginnings of the vegetable plots and gardens. He was first introduced to Cable, who, at three inches, was one of the tallest in height and the primary handler for their projects. Though translucent, Cable had the form of a stocky craftsman with a tool belt, and he showed Null around the grove and their projects. Null felt clumsy, kneeling down to look at the tiny but developing home structures, lanes, and water wells. He often didn't know what to say, other than "good" or "I see." At the same time, their industriousness impressed him.

Cable didn't seem to mind Null's lack of conversation, and after the tours of the latest improvements, Null would sit with Cable and the small beings and they would feast. Music, singing, colorful light displays would follow for several hours. The celebrating made Null the most uncomfortable. He didn't have much to say and often spent time wondering about the next mission, but he was polite to his hosts. Though he still didn't know what to make of what they did, he was courteous and expressed his appreciation.

In an early visit, after a particularly hard mission, Null had come to the grove. What he had done had been successful, but only after a long battle. Null walked up the grove but Cable, who had initially flown happily toward him, drew back, and the small beings all clustered behind Cable. Edgy and irked, Null had been required to come. Cable and the beings' spirits dropped.

Something pulled in Null's heart, and a sway of anger, sorrow, and fear moved through him. He struggled against it at first, but then realized he was exhausted. Cable drew nearer to help, and as Null lay upon the soft summer grass, Cable and the other small light beings began to hover over him, forming a thick blanket of light. As they did, light began to seep into Null's chest. They stayed hovering for several hours. Knots throughout his body began to untie. He realized he was being reworked, and the reworking was for peace. At one point he opened his eyes, and he saw Cable, whose eyes were closed, hovering above him. Ashamed of how he had treated Cable before, he knew how little of himself he had revealed, and now he felt so small next to them.

After several hours, the light beings gradually flew back to their work. Null had sat up slowly, and Cable led him to the river. Null pulled the clothing off his tired limbs and slid his body into the water. He moved his palm across his chest. It was as if his heart and ribs were resettling, and what had covered his soul had broken apart and then come together again in waves. He lay in the river feeling warm, then cold, then hot, then cool. Cable stayed on the banks throughout. There were moments Null opened his eyes to glance at Cable, and Cable would nod, and Null would continue. They remained that way until night.

When Null pulled himself out of the river, Cable had a blanket and dry clothes waiting for him. "You won't see me again, that way. I mean, so rough," Null said, as the two sat by the river. As they two sat, looking at the moving water, and the sun slipping away, Null turned to him and said, "You are a friend."

Cable nodded, a tear sliding down his face, which he didn't wipe away, saying, "We are always here for you, Null, and you are here for us." They sat together without speaking until deep into the night, returning to the grove for a celebration around the fire. The small beings were clustered in small rings. They made up songs to sing at that moment, and there were platters of food they had roasted from the crops they had grown in the gardens.

So now, as he sat next to Eva, he knew she would have questions of why they were here. But whatever questions she had, the gifts the beings gave were soaking into them, and he knew that she needed them, whether she knew it or not.

Eva and Null sat together with eyes closed, and when Null opened his eyes again, he looked toward Cable, who met his glance. Whatever lay ahead, they were now blessed and honored.

Allow me to praise the forest

Allow me to praise the sky

Allow me to praise the echo

Of unbounded endless joy

Unbounded endless joy

They spent the day feasting, eating, lying in the grass, looking up at the sky, enjoying the beauty of the small beings. Occasionally Eva would look at Null. He knew she was thinking of time, but she had remembered to take her cues from him. She thought of Gene, but she also sensed peace here, and when she did, she sent this feeling to Gene. He would be flooded with this as much as she was. Wherever he was, and whatever he was feeling, he would feel this too.

As Eva sat in the grove, Cable came up to her and said, "This is our way. We work and we celebrate." She looked at his impish face and the hammer hung on a loop on a workman's belt around his waist. He was translucent and the light he and the other beings had reminded her of hovering fireflies.

As it grew late, Cable and the other beings drew away to their cottages, and at the very edge of the grove, a narrow space remained for Null and Eva to lay down blankets to sleep. Eva looked at the stars. It reminded her of the days when she grew up with Gene. Null seemed to fall straight to sleep. The previous night she had been forty feet up, and tonight she was on the forest floor, but she was still floating, as if she were above the trees. She let herself think about nothing but the stream of joy that ran through her. Waves of contentment rippled over her body and Null's, and she hoped, over Gene's. They were surrounded by friends. She felt she was floating up into the sky, barely tethered to the earth, and she fell asleep with that feeling, sliding easily into dreams and into waves that nourished her through the night.

#

With each hour, Gene felt lighter. Eva had not returned or called, but Min remembered that Eva might take the drive to Volcano House and stay there for a night or two. She said she would call if she needed anything, and Gene didn't worry. He was doing well, and he wanted to be sure it wouldn't pass; he didn't want to tell Eva he was better, only to wake up and find that the sickness had returned.

He also appreciated the time with Min. She had been so worried the past few months. She was so happy that his appetite returned and that he could walk outside with the dogs. Her face was sweet, heart shaped, and she smiled and laughed at him. The color was returning to her face. She hadn't seen him at ease like this in months. The whole house had sounds of happiness, and the dogs fed upon that too. They roughhoused and played, yapping around both Min and Gene. Even the rain let up so that Gene was able to walk out and clip the ginger that was blooming on the east side of the house. When he did, it began to lightly drizzle, but he smiled; his gait was a little unsteady, but Min saw that his legs were stronger, and his balance was returning. Their good fortune had returned, and she went to the farmer's market and restocked the refrigerator with everything he might want to eat.

CHAPTER 15

UNDER WATER

In the morning, when Eva woke, the grove was quiet. The beings had dispersed into the forest to do their work. Cable had urged Null to stay another night, but Eva was restless, and Null relented, so they said their goodbyes. Cable gave provisions for Null and Eva in bundled knapsacks to take with them. As they put them into their packs, their hearts were pulled by sadness. When they walked to the edges of the grove, Null looked back as Cable receded and flew off to start his work.

Eva had slept well and deeply that night, but she was still a little tired when she woke. She remembered to drink from her flask, and when Null was ready to go, she was too. Null was still carrying the remedy for Gene, and she was glad for that.

She didn't know where they were headed, but Null seemed certain about where to go next. They continued east. They were still in the forest, and traveling was not easy. The roots were overgrown, more than had been in any other place, and the thickness of the trees kept the forest damp and moist and much of the sunlight out.

Despite the sleep and the beauty of the night before, Eva's energy was flagging. Only a few hours into their trek, she began to slow. Her legs began to feel thick and heavy, and she wasn't able to keep pace with Null as she had.

"We've got to keep up," he said at one point after having slowed for her several times.

She pushed herself to go forward, but her skin became flushed, and she had an increasing thirst. She was nearly finished with the violet-colored tea, and her breathing was heavy. Null began to glance back at her and slowed.

Finally, near midafternoon, she asked if they could stop. Null had been edging farther ahead as she fell behind, but he double backed to be with her.

"I don't feel good," she said. "Dizzy." The previous day, she had been filled with calm, and her face had been full of light. Now she reached out to steady herself, dropping her pack. She sat and Null came hurrying back to her. Even though there was daylight, the forest floor was dim from the thickness of the old growth trees, and she couldn't see clearly.

Null put his hand to her forehead, and her head was hot. Her skin color was blotchy and red. He reached for her arms and pushed up her sleeves. She was stained with red splotches; and the abrasions she had the previous day were weeping and raw. What frightened him most were eruptions of skin that looked like webs or broken blood vessels clustered on her arms and throat.

"Null?" She was frightened. Her speech was slurring.

He pulled a blanket from the pack and found a small pocket of overlying roots. The roots were uneven and high enough on one side to create a slightly recessed lean-to. He dropped the blanket down up against the base of the roots and laid her on it so she was now shielded on one side by the overgrowth. She was both flushed and chilled. He covered her with the other blanket and gave her water to drink.

"Is it what they gave me?" She tried to remember what Nora had given her, but her head was fuzzy. She felt so tired. It was difficult to remember all those days ago.

"Eva," Null said to her, lifting her up partially by her shoulders. "At the cottages. Was there anything else? What did they give you?"

"The grain … water," she said, her mouth was dry, her words slurred.

"Other than that? What else? Was there anything else?" He started to lay her back down as she began to shiver.

"The quake. We were outside … we were outside ..." Eva faded.

"Outside? What happened with the quake?" Null held her, but Eva couldn't keep her eyes open, and her head dropped back.

Eva was slipping away, and she began to remember, *it was, it was, something, a bite, no, was it a sting … something hurts, my leg …* and then just as she did after the quake, she slipped away, and she could no longer hear Null.

Null's jaw was tight. The remedy they had given her should have worked, and it appeared it had. She had been in good spirits and had kept up.

This was not what the men had expected. She stopped responding and had gone limp. He loosened her shirt, and began to check her body for more marks, rashes, or bruises elsewhere. She had been favoring an ankle and had a hard time getting in the trees, but he had thought it was fatigue. They had all been tired. He pulled off her shoes and socks and raised the pant leg on her left. Nothing. But then, on her right, he saw it. It must have come upon her in the field, or it had been placed on her when she had lain in the grass after the quake. It was round and blistered, but he knew from every other sign, it was a bite. He only had a few hours now, and no remedy was here. If he could not get it drained, and her body restored, she would not make it. He wrapped her in the blanket, and he was furious. Furious at himself, furious at the mission, and furious that this would happen. *Mistakes, mistakes, mistakes*, he thought to himself. If they had stayed one more night, she would have been more secure in the grove with Cable. He felt blind for a moment. Anger ran through his body, and he wanted to howl. He knelt beside her and asked for mercy. He took a few more moments, silent.

Then he asked for the anger to be burned out of him. He resented all things at that moment, including himself. *The poison of the spider,* he told himself, *is filling me.* With that, he took deep breaths and resolved to take hold. *I can't let it.* He thought of Raila and Nora and he knew what they had done. He knew all in life were essentially good souls, but souls could be overruled by the nature of beasts. He knew the essential decency in beings, but it didn't matter. He had to deal with beasts.

He closed his eyes, clasped his hands together, and for a few moments, felt his body shake. He knew there would be no sanctuary ahead for him if he could not do this. If he failed in this mission, he knew he would have no faith. Despite all he knew, he knew he couldn't keep caring if goodness kept failing. *This is what makes warriors weary*, he thought. *I cannot see goodness fail.*

145

He gathered himself together and made a plan.

He wrapped her more tightly in the blanket, which kept her covered and hidden. Then he set his pack and hers beside her. The roots of the trees that surrounded her on one side would help keep her sheltered. He then dragged long fallen branches to cover the open side of the lean to where she lay. He had to leave for help, and he couldn't leave her exposed. He knew Hugo and Jens would have their attention on him, and from the deepest part of him, he sent out a signal of distress. *I need help* was the message he sent. *Come,* he thought, *come now.*

He realized then that he still had the flask for Gene. There was no reason to think it would help her. There was no certainty that they had made the remedy properly to help Gene. They had two entirely different maladies. He hesitated. It could help her; it could harm her. Null swore to himself. After all these years, no matter what good he did, he always found himself in these moments, in these crossroads of not knowing. With that, the anger that held him began to break. *I don't know much at all.* He dropped to his knees.

With that, he knew that the only thing he could was try. He pulled back the branches off the lean-to, loosened the blanket around her, and lifted her up slightly. He took the flask intended for Gene, opened it, and poured small amounts between Eva's lips. She murmured, but she wasn't conscious. He laid her back down and rolled up the jean leg on her right side. Then with a small blade from his pack, he lanced the blistered bite to try and clean it. He then poured a few drops from the flask into the wound, and then wrapped it in the gauze that she had kept from the kit he had given her. He waited, poured a bit more between her lips, and then capped the flask. He lifted her back onto the blanket, wrapping her in it tightly, with the flask by her side. The sun was going down, and the temperature would soon start dropping.

He held his hand to her forehead and then her cheek. Her skin was chilled and clammy. He gave her one last look, and then replaced the branches that covered the side that was exposed. The earth seemed to swallow her up to protect her, simply branches fallen over roots in a storm. With nothing to carry and with no one he'd have to pace himself with, he began to run. He kept sending that thought to Jens and Hugo, *come, come now.* And he began to run as quickly as he could through the trees. He headed back to the grove, in hopes that Jens and Hugo were already on their way.

#

Hugo had been uneasy all morning. Jens was restless. By afternoon they had decided to pack up and were now running as well, tracking the signs Null and Eva had left, heading in their direction.

#

After their noon break, the small light beings hadn't wanted to return to work on the wells or the cottage buildings. The air wavered, very unsteady to them all, and they began to hum about what to do. Some wanted to keep working, others wanted to stay and prepare provisions for visitors, and others wanted to wait for more signs. Cable decided to keep them together, close to the grove, gathering seedlings from the fields to plant in the gardens.

#

Eva was sinking, deeper and deeper into dark water, and she could feel her hair, starting to lift and sway, surrounding her. Her body wavered, long and languid. Everything was heavy and thick, and she could feel the pressure of water on everything. She moved and drifted and swayed. She was in deep water now, and she no longer needed her lungs. Her chest moved against its weight. She was fully submerged yet breathing.

It took her a long time to open her eyes; it was dim, and she was lying just beneath the shelf of a coral reef. Cold, she floated out where there was more sunlight. She looked at her arms, and they were unmarked now, not as they had been in the forest.

She swam out from beneath the coral shelf, and small schools of fish surrounded her. She brushed through them as she moved. She swam slowly, looking at the sea grass, but it was dim and difficult to see; the light seemed so far away. Then as if called by sirens, she started to hear the songs her mother used to sing.

See the mermaids swim to her

Hear them as they sing to her

>*Be strong*
>
>*Feel loved*
>
>*Take heart*
>
>*Be bold*

She let herself rest and that allowed her to drift in the current. It pulled her back toward the reef where she had been. She had grown so tired. She let it pull her, and she closed her eyes. She just wanted to drift.

To those who watch

From up above

Please tend to those

Who tend to love

Please spare this child

who opens hearts

And light her path with stars

See the mermaids swim to her

Hear them as they sing to her

>*Be strong*
>
>*Feel loved*
>
>*Take heart*
>
>*Be bold*

But she couldn't hear the last refrain, and she wanted to remember it, but everything was fading. She wanted to whisper it to herself to try to remember.

Bring, bring your love
Sing, sing your love
Share, share your heart
Give love to all, to all your love

#

For Null, it was if a conch were being blown or a drummer were summoning the troops in the field. He could only keep running in the direction of help, which now could only be Jens and Hugo, who might know more. He kept sending out the same message, *come, come now.*

CHAPTER 16

TROPHY

Raila and Nora had been traveling away from the open paths and through the thickest parts of the forest, resting in the day, and walking at night. Raila wasn't tired although Nora was. Without much sight for several years, the elder was fed by the night and by the slats of moonlight that fell between the trees. She had cultivated an appetite for the hunt after she had broken off from the others, and she sensed a hunt now.

She and Nora were undeterred by Eva getting away or the thought that someone like Null might be with her. They knew that whatever they had done would stop her, or at the least, slow her until they could find her again. She was near, and they began to chafe against each other, pressing each other to move faster.

They had been one with Hugo, Jens, Null and others for a long time; they had trained with them to move in the forest, track, work with herbs, and be among the light beings. They had loved the work then and been devoted; they had helped people, worked, and grown. But as time had worn on, so had they. They began to struggle with the constancy of the missions and the unevenness of failures and successes. Raila had kept quiet, feeling the younger ones didn't see her as an equal. As Raila and Nora had experienced with the group or alone, what they did was not without risk. At night they began to ponder what the results might actually be. They wondered about the future and how they might live. They wondered about others and their successes. They kept filing away all the thoughts about what they would never have or the close calls they'd had.

"What is all this worth?" Raila said, "That's what I'd like to ask," she said, looking toward Nora pick through greens for tinctures. She tried to see Nora's face. "Have you thought about that?" Then she sat back and laughed, saying, "Does being swept away in mud comfort you?"

At times like these, Nora would just glance away. She continued to work, but she didn't counter her either.

Prone to worry and fear, Nora felt steadier with Raila's certainty. Without it, thoughts trapped Nora. She needed to operate mechanically sometimes, driven by someone else. Her mind churned under the strain, while her insides jerked like rusting bicycle chains on ill-fitting gears, always on the verge of collapse.

Raila wondered about her and started to voice her doubts out loud, even when things were going well. Nora's fears were propelled by victories just as much as losses. Her eyes grew darker. She began to draw away from the group. Her vacancy of will made her vulnerable. Beasts latched onto Nora's spine and fit their own chains around her vertebrae.

Maybe that's what she wants, Raila thought.

At night, when the two women lay on their pallets to sleep, they would sink into a pool of darkness, an oily pool that filled their insides. Steeped in this, they carried this darkness with them, until they left the group completely.

When they decided to divide, Raila urged Nora to mark the occasion. "It's simple," she said, looking in her direction, tilting her head. She handed the shears to her. "It's time for different choices."

Nora sat by a stream, cutting her braids until only ragged tufts remained. She gathered her hair, and like her inner will, she buried it. She knew what Raila thought of her, but inwardly, Nora comforted herself. It can be what I need for now, Nora thought. What I bury, I can retrieve.

"Good," Raila had said, nodding, "No turning back. You've announced it."

In daylight, Nora led Raila, but at night, Raila led. Her senses and confidence were steadier. Once she and Nora were on their own, she learned to plant her feet more skillfully and carefully, between or over the roots, and she could sense groves and herbs at night. The men had underestimated Raila in every way; despite her uneven pace and diminished sight, at night she learned to move faster and farther ahead. It was Nora who would stumble and fall behind. There was a dependence between the two that reversed itself day to night, held together by agitation and fear.

Nora wasn't sure when it began, but the movement and sound of scavengers enlivened them—the sound of nailed claws against bark, the fluttering of hair-thin roach legs when the insects were exposed to light—thrilled them.

"Our little beasts of the earth," Raila said as they walked. "It's not wrong to want to be lords of something, Nora."

Nora looked at her.

"It's not what we rule but that we rule," she said, gripping Nora's guiding arm more tightly.

That night they wound their way around the deepest parts of the forests, avoiding clearings and any patches of light. Nora pointed out the evidence that they were nearing Eva and her companion, which was likely to be Null. They came near a small meadow but swung wide around it, which took longer, but kept them further out of sight. They passed a larger grove and kept walking. As the sky darkened, they stopped to begin their rest. They would wait for night to come.

But as Raila and Nora were laying down their things to settle, the elder stopped. "She's close," she said.

"Where?" Nora asked, "Alone?"

"Alone," she said, and smiled. "We'll keep on."

"But it's still light," Nora started.

Raila didn't like leaning on Nora, but she could feel Eva was near. "It'll be dark soon. The light won't last." With that she reached her arm out to Nora. Nora didn't move or speak, and the two stood, the wind slightly picking up around them. Raila leaned forward again, asking, "Nora?"

Nora looked at her outstretched hand. After a long moment, she gave Raila her arm, and they continued, headed toward where Eva lay, covered by shadows of trees.

#

Raila knew the forest well, and the two were picking up speed. The light in the forest dimmed, and her senses improved. The scents of the night excited her, and she began to move more quickly, and Nora more slowly. They came upon the lean-to suddenly, almost walking directly into it.

Nora let go of Raila's arm and began to pull the branches off the lean-to of roots, and Eva lay exposed, pale, and chilled.

Nora laid a hand to her forehead and looked closer at her.

"She's out," she said, pulling the branches to the side so the elder could approach.

She stood close to Eva and said, "She's near the end."

The two stood beside the lean-to.

Nora spotted the two packs. "Null," she said, "He'll be back. With Hugo or others."

"But not in time," Raila said.

"We can't take her with us," Nora said, taking hold of her arm.

"No," Raila said, "we can't."

Nora was silent.

"We will let things take their course," she said. "That will be enough."

Nora hesitated.

"Take a trophy," Raila said.

Nora looked at her for a moment and then at Eva. Nora did not want to run into Null or any of the others. She took what she wanted quickly and pulled the branches back over the lean-to of roots.

"We need to go. He'll be back, and he'll bring the others," Nora said.

The two began their way out, making a wide loop away from the path of the lean-to and where the others might come. It was getting later now, and they would use no light but would travel by sound and Raila's memory. They drew away as Eva lay in the dark, the lotuses with the coiled-stem serpents riding on Nora's wrist as Raila led the way.

#

Null didn't stop to think; he knew the forest and kept up his speed. He knew that his friends would sense something was wrong. He just didn't know if they would have answers for a remedy or whether it would be in time. He just kept running.

#

Hugo and Jens were racing toward Null, and they weren't alone.

Ann was as strong as any of them; she had the skills of a tracker, the height and strength of a swordsman, and the healing touch of a botanist. But she had no appetite for the constant missions and itinerant life. She had opted very early for sanctuary. Then after five years in sanctuary, she chose family and stability. The easiness of her personality had struggled against the weight and frequency of the missions. Now that her children were grown and her husband content, she sometimes came to assist. She had been gathering herbs with the light beings when Hugo and Jens came upon her. She had missed Null and Eva by half a day.

When Ann had seen Jens and Hugo approach her in the wild grass, she smiled brightly until she saw the urgency in their faces. She was knee deep in the field, her hair shiny yellow, as she gathered and prepared her tinctures. With few words, she immediately fell in with them. This time Ann led, with Hugo and Jens following.

She knew Null had been ready for sanctuary, and she knew what it might do to him if they failed. The three were weary, but they moved as quickly as they could in the increasing dark. They didn't know who else might meet them on the way there.

#

A third of the way back to the grove, Null knew he had run out of time. He hadn't passed anyone, and he had not made the time he needed. He wondered if he had miscalculated. The chance of his saving her if he had remained would have been none. His chance of saving her by bringing others to her was slim, but possible. But such things are not measured in percentages, and this was now about loss. He had not come across Jens, Hugo, or anyone else that could help her.

He stopped running, leaning over to breathe. He paced back and forth and then stood still. Even if it were her last hour, he could sit with her. He had done such things many times, and this would not be new. He decided to turn back.

It was getting dark, and he had lost so much time. Rather than stay on the perimeter, to gain time, he ran in the open. It didn't matter much now. Raila and Nora were heading toward Eva. They were near. He didn't know where Jens and Hugo were, but he knew they could track him, and he counted on that.

#

Eva dreamt she was swimming, but she was swimming among snakes. She was calling out for Null, but he couldn't hear her. She started screaming. The snakes were wrapping themselves around her; they were biting her, twisting around her body, and dragging her downward. One snapped at her wrist, and another raked her forearms with its jaws.

The last thing she remembered was the thought of Gene. She thought of him, just as a snake wrapped itself around the whole of her body and arm, dragging her below.

It was then that Null reached her, pulling the branches aside. He saw that she was breathing but only in shallow breaths. He tried to revive her, but her head dropped back, and she didn't respond. He poured more liquid from the flask through her lips and started calling her name. She didn't respond, and he lay her back down.

Null knelt by her side. He closed his eyes and held her hand, and from the deepest part of him, he asked for peace, for him, for her, for all sentient beings in the world. He had nothing else to fight with, and no one in the flesh to help him.

He sat and held her hand and knew this was the way it would be. She was cold and shivering, and he wrapped her tightly again. He knew he had to be at peace with this. He sat with her and prayed for her, and he prayed for his soul too. He felt her waver, as sheer as fabric, whether to remain in this world or not. He asked her to stay for Gene. He reminded her of the armor the hosts had given her, the cloak that was for her brother, and for the healing water they had made for him.

158

She had now taken those gifts into her own body, and Null told her to send that energy to Gene. He asked if that she could sense her brother and to send him peace. He sat with her in the cold and spoke softly to her. Then he was silent. He had done everything he could, and it was now up to her.

In that quietness, nothing moved around them. Her breathing was shallow and sometimes halting. Null held her hand and let himself fill with light; he remembered how the hosts had covered him with the color of blue and how that had made him feel it was possible to do this last mission. His heart flooded, and he let go of her hand. He closed his eyes and continued to sit beside her. They were now deep into the night.

CHAPTER 17

LOST OR FOUND

When the three appeared, they weren't sure what they had found. Null was lying beside Eva, her body wrapped tightly in a blanket.

Ann had seen many things before. She had been with souls whose time was to leave their physical bodies behind, and she could be with them up to the very last moment. She could reassure them and walk with them to that very last portal. She had also seen when it was too late; too late in the way that someone hadn't made it in time to see a loved one off at the train. Instead, there would only be the blur of glossy boxcars moving, departing as the whistle pierced through the air. But she had also been there at times, when, as if looking down a long corridor, she could reach whoever it might be and tend to that soul. And in that brilliance of light, someone might return earthward or still might choose to dissolve into a sheer brightness of being.

Ann broke from the other two and ran up first. If Eva were still breathing, if she had made it through the night, there might still be a chance.

Ann looked at Null, and unwrapped Eva to feel for a pulse. It was faint but there, and quickly, she took out the tinctures she brought with her. The poison had burned through Eva's body, but it may not have damaged her organs. The tonics might revive her. Ann held Eva's wrist again.

Null had lain beside Eva to give her warmth, and Ann now nudged him aside. He moved, and Hugo offered him water, but he waved him away. He looked at Ann.

"She has a chance," Ann said, looking at her. Null nodded and closed his eyes.

"We'll take over," Hugo said.

"Sleep," Jens told Null as he crawled and leaned against a tree, rubbing his eyes.

Ann checked the bite that Null had lanced, and she cleaned the dressing, pouring a tincture to cleanse her blood. "You kept her alive, Null. We'll see what we can do." Null nodded, with eyes closed.

Jens had walked several feet away and noticed the tracks the other two had left. Both men did not look at Null or Ann.

"They were here," Jens said, partially kneeling to study the ground. "They were here and they left her," he said, and looked at Hugo, who looked down and shook his head.

Ann was busy tending to Eva. The broken blood vessels covered her arms and legs, but the fever had broken, and her skin already less clammy. No one could read the expression on Ann's face.

"Keep feeding her from the flask," Null said, slouching down with eyes closed. "It's not only helping her," he said before falling asleep, "it's helping her brother Gene."

#

After the second day, Gene decided to call Eva, but she didn't pick up on her phone. When he called Volcano House, he found out she had checked in and left her bags, but no one recalled seeing her again. He left a message. The woman in the gift shop had remembered seeing her, so they weren't so worried. It wasn't unusual for Eva to go off, and she often left her phone or had the battery run out.

Min was a little irked that her sister-in-law would cause her brother any worry, but Gene was doing so well. That eased anything else.

That night, Gene went to bed, and he slept deeply, but he began to dream. He dreamt he lay on a cold surface, and when he lifted his head, he saw that he was in a large room, cold like marble. He got up and started calling Eva's name, and the structure was like a tomb with many empty rooms, maze-like, and he began to run, looking for her and calling her. When he woke, he was in a sweat.

He started to make calls and an alert went out. Friends drove out to Volcano House, the art center, and the gift shop. It had begun to rain heavily, and visibility was poor. They were now worried.

#

Eva had never been so adorned in all her life. She had never been waited on or honored in the way she was now. She had never been given such beautiful things. She sat, as silks and heavy satins, as heavy as tapestry, were placed on her body. Her hair was brushed back, and jewels were brought to her. She wore a collar of rose gold, inset with yellow sapphires, and a pin of blue sapphire arrows. She looked down and on each wrist were cuffs of lion heads set with ruby eyes. On her feet were golden silk slippers beaded with jewels and blue stitching. Once her dressing was completed, she gathered herself to return to the great hall. She stepped forward as the doors opened; she was to return to her hosts.

She had never seen so much light before, nor had so much light in her body. She felt translucent and happy, buoyant and free.

All this, the hosts allowed Null to see. He saw her as she entered the hall; he saw the joy lit on her face. They let her see the health of Gene restored. The remedy that had been made for him, they fed to her, and they also fed it into the streams, into the rains, into the water Gene would drink at night. It flowed through him and reached him. It was in everything that grew in the garden and bloomed from the ginger around the house. The darkness had seeped away from him.

CHAPTER 18

DEL DIOS

No one had expected the volume of rain, the sharpness of the turn, or the power outage that occurred up the road. They didn't know why the woman had driven at such speed or why she had skid. But when they found her, there were internal injuries and severe abrasions. Her brother and sister-in-law met the officers at the hospital, and they waited as she lay unconscious. For weeks following, she had no memory of what happened. No one was sure why she had survived; others said it was through grace that she did.

In truth, as she had driven up Volcano, she felt increasingly out of place. She hadn't belonged anywhere for a long time. *You can't suddenly attach yourself to a place as if it were yours, but you can't detach yourself either, as if you had no ties.*

Her memory had deep gaps, but sometimes in recovery, she would have vague recollections of running down corridors or swimming through wave after wave. Sometimes she saw herself pulling her brother out of the waves, or sometimes he would be pulling her above water when she was drowning. Some mornings she would feel the light on her face, and she missed the trees. The memory of a woman would sometimes float over her, with the fragrance of cut herbs and the smell of medicinal tinctures. Or at times she could see the silhouette of a woman standing ankle deep in water at low tide. She could breathe in the fragrance of the sea at moments like these. She also felt a loneliness for someone running ahead of her, moving beyond her among the trees. These would come and go, grow vivid, then fade, then come back again. She knew she had been somewhere, and when she closed her eyes, or sank into sleep, she knew she was finding her way back.

In the next few months, Gene's health would also waver, progress, then falter, then improve again until it finally returned. Eva and Gene recovered together but in different ways. There were gaps in Eva's memory, but there was peace in her eyes. On difficult days she would run her fingers over the bracelet that an officer had discovered far from the wrecked car. It had been battered and twisted, but she found a silversmith who gently molded it back into shape. It had remaining scars like she did, but it reassured her that so many things could be ironed out with the right care. She thought of the lonely day she'd sat outside the gallery before the summit. *The gifts we give ourselves give us strength.* It helped her be at peace as she fought to get her body back and to help Gene build back his.

On some days Min would look at Gene and Eva and feel a pinch to her heart as if she knew they had been somewhere she hadn't, but then they would turn to her, smiling, calling to her, and the fragrance of the ginger would waft in. They had been brought back to her, and it didn't matter how.

In early evening, as Min cooked, the smell of fresh chopped ginger mixed with the scent of rain. Gene and Eva relaxed at the table, and Bruddah Iz's "La' e' lima" flooded the house. They ate, laughed freely, and when the rain came down, they let this all sink deeply as it could into their skin, their flesh, and their bones.

EPILOGUE

Soon after, Null entered sanctuary. Before he left, he gave each an embrace—Ann, Jens, and Hugo—as the four stood together in the fields. His body was tired. He chose a place in the high grounds where the air was dry and cool, and he went into silence. He no longer wrestled with himself about what he had seen. His body was finally letting go. It let go of the tensions of running, of battling, of serving, of fear; he let go of worry, of disappointment. He could grieve now if he needed to. There was no one waiting, or any reason to hold back. He could breathe. He had no other needs to fill. He'd had only one thought; he had wanted her to live. That was a good enough peace for now.

> *scattered from the archipelagoes that birthed us*
> *we declare ourselves*
> *spirit and flesh*
>
> *allowing ourselves to be seen*
> *no longer afraid*
> *of the last step that might lead us*
> *to the illumination*
> *of the moon*

\#

Missing people hurts so much, she thought as she packed her suitcase, *whether they are on earth or not.*

"I'll drive," Gene said that morning as they sat at breakfast.

Min said goodbye at the house and let the two of them go to the airport. She hugged Eva and then waved to them from the driveway, as they drove away from the house.

"Did you write down your appointments?" Eva asked Gene as they turned into the airport, and he nodded. "You don't have to come in," she told him, but Gene drove into the lot, and they parked the car.

I don't know if I can do this, she thought, as she checked for her ticket and ID, and Gene got her rolling bag from the trunk. They walked through the terminal, passing the stands of macadamia nuts and t-shirts, and she glanced at the orchid and plumeria lei hanging on long strings in the refrigerated cases. Early that morning, Min had picked up a ginger lei for her to take with her. It wouldn't last long, but the fragrance helped keep everything in her alive.

They came to the security line. The two of them stood. She let go of her bag, and they hugged each other in a long goodbye, tears running down her face. She would never be ready to let go, and she accepted that. She turned and gave one long last look at him.

#

"These things connect," Eva said to Emi, after Eva returned to San Diego. She looked away, stirring her tea. "If some people don't understand what happened to me—all of what happened—that's okay. I get that. It's unusual." She looked at Emi. "I don't understand it all. It's okay that others don't get it; that shouldn't change loving somebody." She looked down and said "But it can't be that someone so close doubts you and then just tolerates or humors you about what you feel is reality …. It's not about having the same view, but it's also not about ignoring what matters either."

Images of Null sometimes came up in her mind. They weren't clear, but they had a sense of motion; she could see him in the distance, a figure she followed between the trees, and in these moments, she was moving and not thinking. She could feel the tall grass brushing against her legs, and the light scattering itself over her and the figure up ahead.

176

Such peace she felt, such freedom, such assuredness, and such a sense of certainty even though she knew nothing about what lay ahead. She'd had wanted only one thing then. She'd wanted Gene to live.

Emi paused and said, "Just don't be quick to judge. People take time to take things in. I can't say that I get everything you've told me either. But in the end, does it matter what I think? Or for that matter, what you think about what I think?"

Eva looked at Emi, and Emi's expression made her want to laugh.

"I'm serious," Eva said.

"So am I," Emi replied.

On the drive home, winding on Del Dios, the air was warm, and Eva could smell the eucalyptus from the trees. She knew there were still beasts in the woods and beasts in the city and people who didn't feel this could be true. But she was grateful. She didn't know what was ahead, but she had gone after what she couldn't live without. She was lucky. She knew there were things she couldn't explain or control, but there was also a world of light beyond what could be seen, and many had given their all to get her there. What she'd been given had been planted deeply. For all of this, she felt thankful—to the hosts and to Null, to all the guides, family, and friends, to the ones that she loved now, and to those ahead to be loved. What was dark had been lifted up and off of her, and at this moment, on this road, she was certain of two things. The earth and sky had opened, and she knew what it meant in both these worlds to want someone she loved to live.

THE END

ABOUT THE AUTHOR

Pianta is a writer and editor whose work has appeared in journals such as *Adirondack Review, Nimrod International Journal, Ekphrasis, Terrain.org,* and *Bamboo Ridge Press.* She was born and raised on O'ahu, but her grandparents on both sides came from Okinawa. After teaching in California, she returned to live on the Big Island. Her readings often incorporate music and multimedia. Her website is at www.pianta.org.

AUTHOR'S NOTES

Hawai'i is a highly complex place with an intense political and cultural history and present. This novella can't and doesn't address those complexities or intensities. Instead, this is a story about a brother and sister in worlds beyond what we can usually see.

Having said that, it's hard to separate the seen from the unseen and the internal from the external, especially when it comes to identity, culture, and the many selves within us. Sorting these issues out feels like a lifelong pursuit. In terms of Uchinanchu culture , here are some resources and groups: "'Wanne Uchinanchu—I am Okinawan': Japan, the U.S. and Okinawa's Endangered Languages, " Byron Fija and Patrick Heinrich, *Asia-Pacific Journal: Japan Focus,* November 22, 2007; *Chiburu: Anthology of Hawai'i Okinawan Literature*, editor, Lee A. Tonouchi, 2023; Ukwanshin Kabudan, a performing arts and cultural organization; Hawai'i United Okinawa Association; and the Center for Okinawan Studies, University of Hawai'i at Mānoa.

PUBLICATION CREDITS

Poetry excerpts are from "Uchinanchu," *Nimrod International Journal, Fall 2019;* "The Fires," *Acts and Intentions, 2020;* "Rain Poems," *Hawai'i Poems: from there to here,* 2020; "I can write this poem," "Here," "In this world," *Love and Grief in the Time of Ketu, 2020.* Song lyrics are excerpted from "Little Bird," "Spring," "Hear the Mermaids," *Little Bird Songs for Children, CD,* 2020.

RELEASES
Info and trailers at
www.pianta.org

Old Volcano Road
Novella
Ebook and print versions
Available at Amazon

Little Bird: Songs for Children
CD of original acoustic children's songs
Available on iTunes, Apple Music, Amazon, Pandora
Listen to samples at
https://pianta.hearnow.com/

Poetry
Hawai'i Poems: from there to here
Book of new and previously published poems
Available at Amazon

Love and Grief in the Time of Ketu
Poetry chapbook
Available at Amazon

We Don't Know What We Don't Know
Poetry Chapbook
Available at Amazon

Acts and Intentions
Poetry Chapbook
Available at Amazon

All Ends Are Never Ends
Poetry Chapbook
Available at Amazon

Before
Poetry Chapbook
Available at Amazon

A Man in Parts
Poetry Chapbook
Available at Amazon

Short Fiction
Floating
Available at Amazon

More information at
www.pianta.org

www.ingramcontent.com/pod-product-compliance
Lightning Source LLC
Chambersburg PA
CBHW071242130626
46556CB00003B/1133